The Room Upstairs

The
Room Upstairs

MONICA DICKENS

HEINEMANN : LONDON

William Heinemann Ltd
LONDON MELBOURNE TORONTO
CAPE TOWN AUCKLAND

First published 1966

© 1966, by Monica Dickens

Printed in Great Britain by
Western Printing Services Ltd, Bristol

TO G.O.E.
WITH LOVE

THE ROAD FROM Boston to Cape Cod is long and straight
and ruthless. Two black slashes cutting through the sandy
country of pine and scrub oak which never grow to any
size before a motorist throws out a cigarette onto the dry
grass, and levels everything neatly down again.

In winter, the cars carry Boston businessmen in hats
worn straight and true, and women with plastic statues of
the Sacred Heart suctioned to the dashboard. In summer,
the cars are full of families, and trail boats and little
houses behind them.

When the road was made, for the locust families to re-
double their assault on Cape Cod, hills were levelled,
hollows filled, the landscape brought to order. The bare
scrub land is empty, since everyone has gone top-heavily to
the coast, like passengers crowding to the ship's rail.

Because there is nothing to see, nobody looks, and
there are habitual travellers on this road who have never
noticed the yellow wooden house marooned there in the
grass below the embankment.

In the lush months, its ancient trees screen it mercifully

from the summer cars that go by, zip, zip, zip, fifty a minute. It is only in the autumn, when the traffic thins, that the house begins to appear. The oaks reveal one gable. Next week, another. A window heliographing the sun. The sentrybox side porch, as the copper beech begins to lose its claret leaves.

By December, the old house stands nakedly, the broad meadow carpeting the hill behind, furnished with great trees, dark with winter firs. Anachronistic stretch of rolling parkland in a township where people with an acre's garden call it an estate.

The traveller who sees both the house and the high red barn across the road from it realises with a stab of pity that they belong together. On the other side of the highway, the same rolling pasture, the soft track with grass between the ruts, the splendid trees.

In the moment before he is under the bridge and gone, he thinks: Bad luck on *them*, and wisps of phrase like rape of the countryside and the automobile as Moloch go with him up the road, and fall behind.

If he comes back next year and remembers to look again for the yellow house, he will think he was mistaken. What was it he saw? Was it somewhere else? But the red barn is there across the road, and the green slopes of meadow, and the trees.

The house will be gone. Taken away clapboard by clapboard, pane by pane, the banisters done up in bundles, to be set up two hundred miles away, outraged in an alien state.

Why not? None of the family want to live in it any more. Even Laurie. Too much has happened. The headlong cars have the landscape to themselves. The road, in the end, has won.

2

SYBIL'S BEDROOM WAS at the back of the house. On summer weekends when the processions in her head would not let her sleep, she lay on the high bed with her head tied up in a souvenir dish-towel from London and listened to the cars going through her cow pasture, and wondered if she would ever get used to them, as Theo pretended he did.

Sometimes, when it seemed that all Detroit streamed past beyond the trees, she would swing her feet down onto the rug her mother braided in the bad winter of 1910, and go with her old lady's heel-toe shuffle, tapping her fingers along the rail of the staircase well—although she could walk anywhere in the house blindfold—in among the sighing shadows of the front room.

Down into the valley of the wide floorboards and up the other side. She knelt to lean on the window sill and tried to cry, but there are no wet tears at eighty, no beads of sweat.

Only phlegm and urine, both a little out of hand.

Behind her on the bed, flatly quilted with the sunburst patchwork done by Aunt Somebody (the legend was dead at last), Emerson breathed softly, and dreamed of his wedding night.

'It wasn't my fault.' Her dialogues with herself, which at seventy were anxieties and grievances, now often took the shape of justification of things of which no one had ever accused her. 'It wasn't my fault, Papa.'

Elbows on the wide sill, chin on hands, she stared like a witch at the endless indifferent cars, and swore at them with words nobody knew she knew.

ON THE BRIDGE over the road, Laurie stopped the car and they got out to look over the parapet, the metal hot under her bare arms.

'There it is.'

'Is that it?' Jess leaned on the rail, with the cars bolting along below her like coloured bullets, and suddenly the whole thing was disaster. Anticlimax. Coming here to marry him. The adventure dwindled and shrank.

'It's so near the road.'

'I told you. They raped us, simply. I told you.'

'How can you—'

'We can't. My grandfather did. He got used to it, after he won his fight over the compensation. She—never. When they were making the road she used to stand and stare at them. When they graded the banks for seeding, she went out at night and trampled all over them. It was silly. They didn't care. The day they opened this bit of the road for cars, she put on the black she wore at her mother's funeral, dusty and rumpled. I was a kid then. It was summer, and I was here. She went and stood by the fence down there and stared, and people waved to her.'

'I wish—I wish we had been married in England.'

Behind her, the sagas of Gran and the aunts. Dad and his childhood in Watford. The history of her mother's veins. Sagas she had been so glad to run from, before they could catch her by the heel and drag her into the same half life of shopping bags and plastic shelf paper.

Ahead of her now, the saga of these others. So different. Too assured. The Mayflower at the back of it all, reverently, as if it were as long ago as the Crusades.

'Why didn't she move?'

'How could she? It's her home. Mine too, most of my life. Ours maybe, one day.'

4

He turned her to him. His eyes were a surprising clear blue, Nordic eyes, although his hair was very dark.

I don't want to. Jess turned her head away and moved her lips on the words without saying them, a compromise between hurting him and cheating with secret thoughts.

The wooden house was beautiful. Pale yellow, with dark shutters, small casements under the steep gables, a huge brick chimney clinging to the angle of one wing.

Settled low into the trees, at its back the quiet painting of meadow and cows, across its face the bright slashing cars, like knives thrown at a circus.

ALL DAY, PEOPLE had been arriving. It was like the old days, with children coming back from school and college. Their friends in the summer. Weekends with the children married and bringing their children, and people coming in for Sunday lunch, in the days when the tennis court cage was still up, before Theo's ramblers dragged it down into the tangled grass.

'The good old days,' Sybil said brightly to Anna Romiza, who did not see it that way. Anna, who had spent three-quarters of a lifetime in the lesser hotels of Massachusetts, saw people in terms of egg on forks and sheets to whip off no sooner than on, and nasty stains on the carpet. She had been shifting the dust around at

Camden House since she came to live with her son four years ago, and was more disenchanted than feudal.

Thelma had come from Philadelphia. Without her second husband, since no one liked him. Her mother could not always remember his name. No one knew whether Laurie's father would be there tomorrow. No one was even sure where he was.

Sybil's son John had come, garbed with city, unrelaxed, a dry white line on his lip from stomach tablets. His wife with her famous menopause, and the two girls, mysterious under their tents of hair, grubby toes clutching the sandal thongs like apes.

Sybil's brother Ted had been here for a week, with his linen hat and his lunatic goggling grin, his head wobbling like a spring-necked doll set going by a child's finger. He was in his old room over the kitchen, among the sewing machines and padded dummies, and every time he tottered down the back stairs, Sybil thought the old fool would fall and break a hip, and she would be stuck with him for months.

Poor Mary would be here tonight. 'Who will meet the train?'

'Time that woman learned to drive,' John said.

'At forty-six?' His daughter snorted. 'I'll go.'

'You don't have a licence.'

'Who cares?'

This year, it was her stock answer. Last year, it had been: So sue me.

The house was filling up with family. It seemed odd to Sybil that she wanted them when they were not there, but felt little for them when they came: always more of a nuisance than she remembered, older, plainer, more censorious. Sometimes they talked about her as if she were

6

not there. Sybil did not mind. It gave her the opportunity to hear what they said about her. She's getting a bit . . . someone said. Well, let them think so.

Laurie was the one. Laurie was the only one she really wanted.

The thought of him being married tomorrow shot through Sybil like hot needles. *I hate her.* She went to the poxy mirror behind the door of the broom closet to see her pouchy old face drawn down into the saucer of her lower lip. With her gaunt nose and bristly grey and ginger eyebrows, she could look very ugly when she tried. She stuck out her tongue, inspected the bluish knot of vein on one side, put it back, and champed on the resurrected taste of the lobster John and Althea had brought for lunch.

She did not hear the car. Laurie flung open the back door, calling out: 'Here she is! Where are you? Here she is!'

I hate her. Sybil nodded at her reflection calmly, her lips composed, and turned with her arms wide in welcome.

Laurie was twenty-six, but looked less in shorts, bare legs and sneakers worn through at the toes, his long London haircut flung about by the drive in the open car. He held by the hand a girl of his own height with square shoulders and straight thin legs, a nervous smile, and eyes under the sand-coloured forelock at once honest and surprised, as if surprised at her own honesty.

7

Lost. Uncertain. Not at all what I thought.

'She's just what I thought she'd be! Welcome to the family, my dear.'

She moved towards them, deliberately tottering a little in a bid for benevolence, abandoning without ever having donned it the role she had planned. She would not be the grandmatriarch, formidable, austere. She would be the frail old lady who could depend on this nice English girl for love and attention, as she depended on Laurie.

'Emerson's room!' The grandmother opened the door on a low, cool room with musty print wallpaper and a few bits of venerable furniture leaning inwards with the tilt of the floor. The bed was a four-poster, with a frame but no canopy, and a beautiful patchwork quilt, sprouting threads.

'He was my father's friend, Jess. He stayed here often, you know.'

She crossed the room and stood by the window, shaking her fist at the cars. She made a fist in an odd way, with the thumb straight up and the fingers flat on the palm, shreds of magenta polish on the long spatulate nails.

Then she leaned to look through the low casement, and pressed her face for a full minute against the screen. She turned round, the end of her nose chequered with the pattern of the screen wire, and went on unconcernedly:

'He slept here the night before his marriage. In this room. So did I. When John was going to be married, I put him in here. Thelma too. Well, it was her room then anyway. Poor Mary will never marry now. I don't know whether Emerson was disappointed.'

She said this so chattily that Jess felt foolish, having to ask: 'The room isn't—isn't haunted, or anything?'

'No, my dear. But it's his room, after all. I told you that. Naturally you can sometimes hear him breathing.'

OF COURSE, THEY blamed her for all the fuss in the night, when the girl woke screaming, and had to be given a sleeping draught, and looked a wreck on her wedding day.

'Making up tales like that, Mother,' Thelma said. 'You are naughty.'

To be called naughty, like a child. Just because no one had heard the breathing, that didn't make it any less true. Did Nigeria not exist because none of them had ever seen it? Oh yes, Robert did, that time he brought home a croco-dile skin, and Marma had the shoes and purse made.

TWO DAYS AFTER Laurie and Jess were married, Sybil fell down the back stairs and broke her thigh.

She fell over a small pile of laundry that she had left on the second step with a warning memo to herself that it might trip Ted.

But Ted was in bed and asleep when it happened. She had just looked in on him, as she always did, to satisfy herself that he was still alive. He looked dead enough, with his jaw dropped and his half-open eyes rolled back into his skull, but the blanket was moving up and down, and he was snoring softly.

On the table, a child's nightlight, made like a little train, shone a blue Christmas bulb through the driver's cab, so that Ted could find his cookie jar, or his slippers, or his glass of water, or any of the things that punctuated his sleeping and waking through the night.

At the other end of the room, which had become the sewing nook after Ted left home, a pale figure kept guard. He had put his seersucker jacket and his linen hat on one of the chesty Edwardian dummies.

'Good night, dear,' Sybil said, either to her brother or the dummy, whose shape reminded her of her mother. It had been Marma. It had worn the rose brocade when they were going to the Inaugural Ball, and Miss Hatch was shut in there with it for days with her mouth crimped round the pins.

Sybil shut the door softly, turned to go down and make herself a hot malted, fell over the laundry, and woke hours later with no memory of what had happened.

Why am I lying on the floor? Get up, old woman, and get to bed. The first flexing of her muscles to rise told her to stay where she was. I've broken my leg. Well, it has happened at last. As soon as you turn seventy, everyone starts to warn you about ice patches and wet doorsteps and scatter rugs. When you're eighty, they would put you in a chair, if they could, and wheel you everywhere. Is this the end then? End of freedom and doing what I like? Perhaps I shall die, lying here like a fallen tree; then they'll be sorry.

But Laurie will weep for me. Not that girl. She thinks I am a witch. She'll bury me and move into this house, you'll see, and take down all my pictures.

What room is this? Unfamiliar from this angle. Because she could not raise her head without awakening pain somewhere, she turned it from side to side and saw, in the sallow pause before daybreak, table legs, a thicket of chairs, a button. The rubber spool with a bell in it she had bought for the cats at Christmas. The white underside of a cat bowl, crusted with old fish. A cat itself, crouched with its front paws folded, watching her without emotion.

The kitchen then. Beyond the cat, the dearly beloved claws of the old black iron stove, which wore the bright curlicued label Priscilla welded onto its wide breast, like a horse on a merry-go-round.

Squinting up, she saw, by the luminous clock at the back of the white electric stove that had ousted Priscilla, that it was four o'clock. She must have been out nearly five hours. No wonder her head hurt worse than her leg. Naked under the rucked up nightgown and robe, it lay alongside the other, identical with ridge of bone and flabby calf spread on the floor. But the left foot was turned out like a broken doll.

Her head fell back. 'Ted!' she called, as loudly as she could with her throat stretched. 'Ted!' But you could fire a gun in his room and the old pantaloon would never hear. Her eyelids dropped, and she slept again, with a dream of childhood, and woke still in the dream, walking beside her father through the wet meadow grass, to milk a cow.

Her summer cottons are loose, because she has too much figure for eleven, but the wide apron sash shapes her waist, and feels comfortable and full of purpose. Marma doesn't like her to milk the cows. She says she would put bloomers on them if she had her way. Jack, or someone like that, said: 'Why not the bull?' and she made out she didn't hear. She won't look at the bull. She hardly ever comes up to the barn anyway, and it's months since she went up the hill to the nursery, or even to the pond. She tells Papa he is out of his mind to keep on at the outdoor work when there are men to do it.

By grace divine, O Nature, we are thine. That is one of the things he says.

A step from sun into twilight. The barn is sweet with hay and dung and cow's breath. Of humblest friends, bright creature, scorn not one.

Flat on her back on the black and white squares of the

kitchen floor, Sybil lay quietly, tag lines of Wordsworth reeling idly through her head, and the minor naturist poets with whom her father seasoned her childhood.

Now with violets strewn upon her, Mildred lies in peaceful sleeping. All unbound her something tresses and her throbbing heart at rest. And the something rays of moonlight, through the open casement creeping, show the ring upon her finger, and her hands crossed on her breast.

If it was Monday, Anna would come. Nothing to worry about, except to get the robe pulled down before Anna walked in the back door. She would come through the little hallway where the old hats and coats mouldered, looking cross because it was Monday. Then she would scream, and clap a black hand over her mauve lipstick. Anything out of place made her scream, even a garbage bag rifled by cats, so the sight of Sybil stretched out on the floor should make her really yell. And Ted would wake at last, and feel badly for having slept.

But Anna could not walk in, because the door was bolted. She would think Sybil had gone visiting, and go away.

'Ted! Ted—help me!' All my life, I've looked out for him. Lied for him to Marma. Carried notes to that girl down by the fish pier, and now look.

Oh Lord, help me—why do I always call on you last?

The door at the top of the stairs creaked open, and slippers shuffled out.

The turn of the stairway hid her from the upper hall, but she called with all her strength, and beat on the floor with her hands. She raised such a racket that the cat got up and walked away, but Ted went on towards the bathroom and shut the door. When he opened it again, she was shouting and sobbing with distress and exhaustion,

13

but his feet went slop, slop past the head of the stairs, and his bedroom door closed. Sybil had just enough strength to register that he had forgotten to flush the toilet again, before thought was blotted out.

WHEN UNCLE TED woke with the taste of soda crackers in his mouth, and found that it was gone nine and Sybil had not come raging in to dash the curtains apart and tell him he was lazy, he felt quite annoyed.

Nine o'clock come and gone, and no juice. She was getting very selfish, that girl. Too much fuss made of her at the wedding, with toasts drunk, and that dam' fool congressman making over her.

You look like a bride yourself, my dear Mrs Prince. Well, he could tell him how old she was, Ted thought grimly, and went cautiously downstairs to see about getting his orange juice, since nobody cared whether he lived or died.

She wouldn't let him into the icebox, but—hey there, what's this now?

Turning the corner, Ted almost fell down the last few steps, and knelt over his sister on all fours, calling to her to wake up. What to do, if she was dead? He was afraid of the telephone. It rang, as she opened her eyes. She stared blankly into his face for a few moments, creepily not like Sybil.

The ringing went on, understanding flicked into her

14

eyes, and she said: 'What's the matter, you deaf or some-thing?'

'Yes.' She was the old Sybil, not scary.

'Get the telephone.'

'You know I—'

'Ted, for God's sake!' He saw then that she was hurt. Her face was full of pain, her lips stiff and bloodless. After she woke, she had begun to shiver, although the kitchen was flooded with sun.

He put out a hand to pull down her bathrobe, but she clutched at his arm and cried out: 'Don't touch me!' He pulled himself up by the post at the bottom of the stairs, and went in his pyjamas into the other room where the telephone squatted, daring him. He picked it up carefully and pressed it hard against his good ear, which had been functioning at half speed for years.

'That was Anna.' He came back into the kitchen quite jauntily, for he had managed a telephone conversation without messing it up. 'Her grandson has the measles. She isn't coming in today.'

'Is she going to get help?'

'Why I—I don't—' Jauntiness dropped away.

'Didn't you tell her what happened?'

'I don't know what happened,' he said plaintively. 'I didn't tell her anything. She hung up.'

'Ted.' Sybil turned her head sideways to look at him. Her eyes were shrunk to a dark glitter, like washed pebbles. Her voice was weak but familiar, the voice for trying to get something into his head. 'I've broken my leg. You've got to get help. Doctor Matson. The police. The fire station. Anyone.'

'I can't use the dial.' Tears began to squeeze out of his eyes because he was so useless.

'You can.' Her teeth were in and her pale mouth firm. She stuck out her jaw at him. 'Dial 0. Tell the operator to get a doctor. Anyone.'

Yes. Yes. He could do it. Almost running, with bent knees and toes out, he hurried back across the passage, picked up the earpiece again and put a finger like a trembling wad of putty into the dial. Nothing happened. The shrill hum of no one went on into his good ear.

The telephone was on a low table. He picked it up to peer at the dial. M. N. O. He tried again. Still no one. Hurry, Ted, hurry. There's only you. His hands were shaking so much now that he could not turn the dial. With a crash, the telephone slipped from him, and bounced off the edge of the table onto the floor.

'What happened?'

He pulled it up a little way by the cord and looked at it, his lips moving in and out, his ear aflame from the receiver jammed so tight, then he let it fall and dropped the other piece after it. It wasn't humming any more. Ted went back as far as the kitchen door.

'I dropped it, Syb.'

'Dear God.' He thought she sobbed. 'Try again.'

'I can't. The front seems to be broken off.'

'Oh God,' she sobbed, and rolled her damp grey head from side to side on the floor. 'Oh God, help me. Help me, Lord, have mercy.'

She called no more on Ted to help her, but he would. He would and he could. He took coats from the hooks in the back hall, old coats, Theo's Donegal, a raincoat that had been to Europe, and covered her, tucking them under her chattering jaw. Swift as thought, he folded a towel and slipped it under her head.

'Stay there!' he commanded. 'Don't move.' Her eyes

16

were closed now, and he did not know if she heard him, but he could hear himself and see himself, the saviour hero, and he felt himself a foot taller and strong as a young bull.

To the rescue! He threw a gallant salute at the inert bundle on the floor, turned smartly down the passage and through the long front room. The nearest house was far away, but just beyond the wide windows, the cars flashed sunlight back through the trees. Stop!

In the hall, he tore through the coats in the closet, showering wire hangers, and pulled his own haphazard over his pyjamas. A brief struggle with the bolt of the front door, and then he was out and stumbling down the hill, clutching his coat round him, his slippers soaked already, breath rasping.

At the bottom of the meadow, he stood against the fence and waved and shouted at the cars on the embankment. Sometimes the rushing faces looked down at him. Once or twice, in a slower car, there were smiles, and someone waved.

'God damn you!' Clutching the fence with one hand, he shook his fist and raved at them, a mouthing puppet, rag doll in baggy pyjama legs.

There were not many cars going this way. On a Monday, most of the cars were on the other side, headed away from the Cape. God damn! He cursed them too. They could see him there with his wild white hair and his pyjamas. Why in hell didn't they stop?

Take it easy, Ted. The raving old man gave place again to the cool hero. This isn't helping Sybil. With calm pride at his resource, he broke a long branch from a tree and tied to the end of it the enormous white handkerchief which was stuffed half in and half out of his pocket.

'Stop!' he whispered. He had no voice to shout any more. He waved the flag, holding the stick with both hands, bending his body to it.

It was an ancient mariner and he stoppeth one of three. Four, five, six cars went by. Someone pointed, a child waved and laughed out of the back of a station wagon receding. In a small green car, the driver turned his head, passed, slowed, stopped, backed the car up a little, then got out and ran back along the grass verge. He was young, in a plaid jacket, his long morning shadow flung down the slope.

'What's the matter?'

'I need help,' Ted called up, trying to keep his cracking voice heroic. 'Please help me. Get a doctor.'

'I am a doctor,' the young man said, as if he were as surprised to hear it as Ted.

3

SYBIL NEARLY DIED.

'I nearly died, you know,' she told Montgomery Jones complacently.

'I know. I was there, remember?'

She shook her head. She could hardly remember what had put her in the hospital, and nothing of being very ill, except odd scraps of dream, like Laurie's face magnified three times its size, and Mary's whine, somewhere unseen: I have a train to catch.

It was all a tangled tale, punctuated by pain, bells ringing, brief unrelated voices that did not fit. That was why she must be on the lookout for people telling her lies about it. Even this young Doctor Jones, with his crooked nose and his bright humorous eye, who was much more fun than the nurses with their sterile, babyish jokes, even he had his story. Just happened to be driving by. As if anyone could believe that. However, he was perfectly charming, and Dr Matson could come begging for business, as long as Jones stayed in Plymouth. Sybil had half a mind not to pay old Matson's last bill, because he was not there in her extremis, although actually no one had sent for him, since Montgomery was in charge.

Laurie said that her bills had all been paid, but that could not be so. He'd never find them all. Even she could not remember where some of them were.

Now that she was learning to walk again, pushing the rubber-footed metal frame ahead of her like a criminal in a portable dock, she would wander into the rooms up and down the corridor, and tell the other patients the story of My Accident. The details shifted, but the central theme of heroics held fast.

There I was, running to get help for my brother, who was ill. He's eighty-two, you know, poor old soul. . . .

'I didn't let you down,' Ted said, visiting, hat on knee, nervous of the nurses. 'I did it for you, Syb.'

'Did what?' With her best New England aspirated W.

'Got the doctor.'

'What doctor?'

And Thelma, who had brought poor old Ted to see her, because they had all expected her to die, said: 'That Montgomery Jones, lucky for you. No knowing what Uncle Ted would have done, or you either, if he hadn't stopped his car.'

Oh, they were all out to fool her, just because she couldn't remember anything about that day. Or was it night? There was a vague, disturbing memory of Marma's dummy, hatted, glimmering in the blue light from the little train.

'But there is nothing wrong with me now,' she told Montgomery, who was sitting on the bed next to her bad leg and reading her newspaper. 'And I want to go home. Indeed, I must go home. There are a thousand things to do. The cats—'

'The cats are in the barn. Laurie has told you that a hundred times.'

He was young enough for asperity, not always the careful patience with which the middle-aged insulted age.

'But that house can't stand empty. It's not that kind of house, Montgomery. My father built it over a hundred and twenty years ago, for his bride. Once before he died—not the time he did die, but the time he thought he would —he made me promise it would never be sold. Ted never cared for it that much, and the others—my stepbrothers and sisters—they thought Plymouth was dead.'

'It isn't now. You can't drive down the street in summer.'

'Oh, summer people. They don't count.'

Cherish my house, Papa had said. She thought of all the empty rooms, holding their breath. The floorboards trying out a creak to see if anyone was there. The waiting furniture, resting a leg on a matchbox or a wad of paper, like stabled horses.

'I must go back.'

'I don't think you should live alone, Mrs. P.'

'Why not? I have for years. Just because I broke a leg doesn't mean I'm senile, whatever Thelma has been telling you.'

'You could have a nurse for a while. I know a nice woman who—'

'Who wants a job. I don't need a nice woman. I'm not a baby.'

'I don't trust that leg yet.' He laid a clean bony hand on the sheeted hump of it as if he owned it, which he did, just about. Sybil did not count the surgeon. 'You could spend a few weeks in a nursing home, maybe, till you're stronger on your feet.'

'Thank you,' she said. 'I'm not ready to go yet. They take over all your savings, and then kill you off quite soon, so they can have the money. Didn't you know?' For a doctor, he was terribly naïve.

LATER, WHEN LAURIE and Jess came from Boston, where they lived in an apartment on the Cambridge side of the river, Montgomery took them to the hospital cafeteria to have a talk among the paper cups and doughnuts.

'She wants to go home,' he said. 'And she's ready to go home. But not alone.' He was a tall young man, who stooped over tables. He looked up at Laurie from his stoop, stirring his coffee with a wooden tongue depressor.

In the hospital, she was Mont's problem. Let loose, her independence destroyed, perhaps forever, by that pile of laundry on the second step, she was the family's problem. Laurie's problem, Jess thought. And so mine.

Thelma was in Philadelphia, sponsoring art shows with her new-married money. John was always All Tied Up in the New York office, or the Bridgeport plant, or the status house at Darien, where Anthea and the girls had learned to live most of life without him. Mary was in New Jersey, teaching kindergarten children not to read, because reading started in the first grade.

Laurie was with a law firm in Boston, near enough to come often. He cared much more than anyone else, Jess knew. More like a son than a grandson.

22

But if I am going to be jealous of an old woman of eighty at this stage of my marriage, I'd better go back to England and cut Gran's toenails, as a penance. You don't know what marrying is, Mother said. But I do. It is unbearable heights and unbearable depths and long, long, stretches that are either content or boredom, you don't ask which.

'She rejects the idea of a nurse,' Mont said, pursing his lips, trying to look like a family doctor.

'Too expensive anyway, on top of what she's paid here.'

It was Laurie who took care of Sybil's money now, and the others gladly left him to it.

'Do what you think best,' his mother had said. 'Thank God we have a lawyer in the family at last.'

They had opened Camden House one weekend when Thelma came up, and the three of them stayed there. Jess had made Laurie lock the door of Emerson's room. She would not go in that room again. If they ever had to live in this house, she would have the door sealed up and wallpapered over, like that Paris hotel where the woman died of plague.

What happened? they had kept asking her. What happened to you? But she did not say, even to Laurie. The grandmother had not asked what happened.

That weekend, Jess had cooked, and swept up some of the dust that the cleaning woman was supposed to have been taking care of all these weeks. The cows belonging to the farmer who rented the pasture and barn had broken some fences, and Laurie went out in the rain to mend them. When Jess came out to him, they lay under the pattering tent of the huge weeping beech tree, and later carved their initials intertwined on the elephant bark, where his boy's carving was, and all the family names,

23

the older ones swollen and spread as the tree grew.

Thelma had spent most of the time complaining about the weather, and throwing the cats out as soon as Jess let them in, and wandering about the house condemning the furniture and pictures and ornaments, although she had grown up with most of them.

'Do whatever you think best,' she said, when Laurie wanted her to go through Sybil's desk with him.

'Well, she's your mother.' He screwed up his face and ran his hands through his soft black hair.

'Go on and make like a lawyer,' Thelma said sternly. 'Power of Attorney. Your father would be proud of you.'

Laurie's father was an alcoholic, drowning without trace somewhere in Europe. Laurie never made jokes about him. Thelma did.

'She had a fit when I said nursing home,' Montgomery told them. 'And I figure there's no one in the family she'd live with, even if they would—if they could have her, so—'

'We'd have her with us,' Jess heard herself saying, 'if there was room in the flat.' Would she have said that if there had been?

'Sweet.' Laurie gave her a smile she did not deserve. 'But she'd never leave Camden House. She wants to be buried there, on the hill where my great grandfather had his plants. I think there's a law against it.'

'The coloured woman she talks about. Would she stay with her?'

'Anna Romiza? It's all she'll do to come in and clean.'

'You'll have to find her a companion, a housekeeper, something like that.'

'How?'

'Advertise or something. I don't know.'

They both looked so defeated, although it wasn't Mont's problem, that Jess said quickly: 'I'll do it. I'll find someone.'

THE OTHER GIRLS in the office took a long lunch break to get their hair done. Jess washed her short light hair herself, but she could take longer too, and dash back across the river to the flat to interview people in the lunch hour.

But there was no one to interview.

She put advertisements in all the Boston papers, and the Plymouth paper as well, but the only reply was from a desperate woman who asked her to send on the names of anyone she rejected, because she would take just about anybody at this stage, for her stepfather.

Sybil had eventually agreed to a housekeeper. She would not have taken it from her children, or from Laurie, but Montgomery decreed it, and she took it, as long as it was not called a companion. 'I am my own companion. I don't want her around me all the time, making silly conversation.'

A housekeeper. Now that she had agreed, she could not wait. She telephoned Jess every morning at a quarter to seven, because the nurses woke her at six, to say she could not understand the problem.

'There must be dozens of women looking for a good home. Why, they should almost pay me to take them.'

'The only one I've heard from, Gramma, wants a hundred and twenty dollars a week, a separate apartment with television, and free keep for her fifteen-year-old boy, who is retarded.'

Restlessly, Sybil roamed the hospital corridors, in and out of the rooms of the well and the ill and the boarded up old bodies that were neither well nor ill; sometimes with a stick, sometimes with the metal walker, if she felt regressive. She would not do crosswords, nor read, nor watch television, nor do anything but fuss about getting out. 'And believe me,' Mont told Jess, behind Laurie's back, 'there is no one in this hospital who won't raise a cheer when she does.'

No companions. No housekeepers. Not one.

Companion-housekeeper wanted for elderly lady in beautiful country home near Plymouth. Good salary to right person.

In three weeks, Jess spent over thirty dollars on her attractive offer. No one cared.

When the call came from Mrs Melia Mulligan, who would go anywhere, do anything, love anybody, as long as she could bring her little dog, just like a child to her, Jess called Laurie at his office excitedly and said: 'I'm going to take her, whatever she's like.'

'Very well. Thank you. That is good news indeed.' The juniors were not allowed to take personal calls.

'I love you.'

'Thank you. Yes. I appreciate it.'

'MULLIGAN?' SYBIL RAISED her bony nose like a retriever, and scented the idea of Mrs Melia.

'Well, but all the charm of them—'

'She'll not have long to charm me,' Sybil said. 'Just till I can go without my stick. Does she want the earth?'

'Not too bad. Laurie will pay her for you, if you like.'

'I'll pay her. That way, she'll always know who's boss.'

BUT THERE WAS no question of Melia Mulligan not knowing.

She was plump and unpretentious, with long pocketed aprons, and hair drawn neatly back into a small colourless bun like an English muffin before toasting.

After her first shock at seeing the black Priscilla stove— 'Don't tell me I've to cook on that!' recoiling as if the kitchen were alive with roaches—she made purring acceptance of everything in the house, and thanked Sybil, almost with tears, for her room over the side porch, which had been done up with new curtains and bedspread by Jess.

She brought a hooded basket for the small dog, and covered its cushion with a piece of material left over from the curtains. Tiger was a sharp-nosed weakling with huge waxy ears, who shivered a lot because he had no hair, only a sort of suede pile on his rodent body. He sat in the basket most of the time, peering out of the opening like an owl in a tree, and was no trouble to anybody.

Melia was amiable and sweet spoken, with a ready

27

laugh and a snatch of song to lighten all tasks. She cleaned the windows, and tore down curtains to have at them with bleach and starch, and made little creamy puddings in glass dishes for Sybil, and carried up trays when she went to bed early, which was often, for she still found herself easily tired.

She swept leaves from the walks when the man did not come, and struck geranium cuttings before the frost knocked out the straggled plants, and even turned out all the old medicine bottles from the cupboard at the top of the stairs. On Anna Romiza's mornings, the coffeepot was always on the go, and banana bread, with so little left to do that Anna revised her opinion of the job and stopped telling her son it was time his poor mother retired.

Sybil was not allowed to drive, 'for a while', they said, but they had been trying to get her off the road for years. However, Mrs Mulligan drove Sybil's car neatly and safely, and they took little trips to admire what Melia called the foliage, and pottered round the supermarket together, with Sybil pushing the shopping cart to keep herself steady, while Melia popped back and forth with things from the shelves, asking: 'Do you fancy this, my lady?'

People who met Sybil in the town, where she knew everybody except newcomers of ten years or so, exclaimed at how well she looked.

'The word went out that you were dead,' Maud Owens told her bluntly, eating Melia's cake, lifting her skirt to warm her bony knees at Melia's red-hot fire. 'But you look better than ever. I wish someone would find a Mrs Mulligan for me. I'm sick of cooking for myself. And I'm sick of frozen pies and T.V. dinners. That's a cute little dog too. Here fellow—here stoopid.'

There was nothing cute about Tiger really, but he was part of the picture of cosiness. He was Melia's child, who slept on her bed, and shared her meat, and had never even seen the label on a can of dog-food.

When she was alone, before My Accident, Sybil, like Maud, had seldom bothered with a proper meal. But Melia loved to cook meat, and could do things with potatoes and pastry that began to put back some of the weight that Sybil had lost on the genteel hospital food.

When Montgomery Jones discovered what fine meals they were having in the yellow house down there in the hollow between the road and the rising pasture, his little foreign car would frequently nose down the zigzag driveway at supper time. He was cooking for himself in an elongated apartment over his office, 'till I can find a wife', though he was not looking, as far as Sybil could see.

'Just stopped by to see how it's going, Mrs. P.,' and Melia would come through from the kitchen, rosily beaming. 'It's a funny thing, Doctor, but I've a roast in my oven only wants ten minutes to carving.'

LAURIE AND JESS found Montgomery very much at home, mixing martinis for them when they arrived on Friday night for the weekend.

He stayed for dinner. 'He always does,' Sybil said, and afterwards she brought out some of the old blackberry brandy, and they played cards before the fire. When Jess helped her up the stairs to bed, she was able to look Emerson's green door in the face for a moment, before turning quickly away.

'You mustn't be afraid, Jess dear,' Sybil clung to the rail above the stair well, getting back her breath. 'Come into the room with me,' she said, more gently than she had yet spoken to Jess. There was a tenuous suspicion between them still. Not dislike, and not quite jealousy, but strangely to Jess, she was the only one who made her feel an alien, although Sybil was less American than anybody else.

'Come with me.'

'No.'

'Come.' Sybil rapped her cane on the floor. She had said she would have Melia only until she could abandon the cane. It was beginning to be doubtful whether she would abandon either of them. Melia had turned her into a cosseted old lady. The cane had provided her with a whole new stock of old lady gestures. She could swish with it at the tall dying weeds along the driveway, point it at the cars like a gun, sit with it between her knees in a witch's pose, chin on her hands curved over the handle, thump its rubber tip to emphasise or command.

Gently, for she was not imperious, in spite of the cane, she took Jess's hand and pulled her to the door of the front bedroom.

'Open the door.'

'You open it.'

Because the house was not square any more, the door sloped and stuck a little. Jess caught her breath as Sybil pushed briskly, then let it out on a short laugh. What had she expected to see? The room was just the same. Faint breath, like an old book, from the wallpaper whose faded pattern did not fit the ceiling line. The shining black fire-place, with the glassed over picture some child had painted on the wood above. The posted bed, with the soft rays of colour, quilted like the sun in silks and prints and chequered gingham.

Jess put a hand on the bed, and then sat down. The terror of the night before her wedding seemed far away. Had she imagined it? Had it been a dream?

After switching on the light, Sybil crossed to the window, stepping carefully on the uneven floor. The lights of a car flooded the sky between the bare branches of the trees, and she shook her fist at it ritually, with the thumb up. She turned round, still wearing her road grimace, and let it broaden into a smile.

'You see. There is nothing to be afraid of here.'

'But you said . . . you know . . .'

'Oh yes, I know,' Sybil said matter of factly, and it did seem absurd to imagine fear in the homely, lighted room.

But Jess had to ask, whispering it so that there was a chance that Sybil might not hear, and she would not have an answer: '*You know there is a ghost.*'

'The only ghosts in this house are happy ones, my dear,' Sybil said, quite casually, as if she were speaking of the wiring, or the drains.

'OF COURSE, THERE aren't really any ghosts here at all,' Laurie said downstairs, 'happy ones or sad. She makes them up to give the house more antiquity. Don't let her scare you, darling. She's only trying to impress.'

'I'm not scared.'

Mont moved across the sofa to let her sit by the fire, and said: 'I should think it's rather hard to impress an English person with anything less than five hundred years old. Or scare them.'

'I was though.' Jess looked at him, her eyes round. One day she was going to tell someone. It might be Mont.

'Not of the ghost,' Laurie said. 'She was scared of marriage. That's why she yelled. No one's ever been frightened here. Except my poor Aunt Mary, and she'd be frightened in a washroom. It's always been a happy house, full of family, and people at home with each other. Not like the house at Northampton, when my parents were together. It bulged with hate. You could see it as you walked down the street. I always came here whenever I could. When I was at Harvard, Mother was courting whats-his-name, so I could come here all the time. I brought all my friends, and they used to feel it too. Everyone was always happy here.'

And Jess was happy that weekend. More steadily happy than she had been since she and Laurie had known each other. Even in London, with all the first excitement of love, it had been too unpredictable. Experimenting, misjudging, saying things too quickly, not guessing they would hurt.

Until Laurie, the boys she had known had hurt her. They had all been too casual to let her hurt them. Laurie was vulnerable, wary as an adolescent. It had been baffling at first to lose him suddenly, without knowing why.

And those first months at the flat with someone else's furniture and saucepans, nothing they had acquired together, setting up provisional house like strangers almost, because there had never been enough time in London for discovery. Finding joy. Finding disappointment. Disappointed with him for being himself and not a projection of her. Disappointed with herself because marriage did not automatically sweeten and soften her, as she had expected. Watching from the high window to analyse her feelings when his head came out of the cave of the subway. Getting out of bed and going into the other room in the dark, because she dared not let him wake and find her crying stupidly for England.

That weekend at Camden House, everything was right and clear, and they were perfectly in love.

November was like September, with sun and birds and soft damp earth, and Laurie and she wandered all over the land, enchanted with each other and the easiness of life together. He showed her all his childhood places. The rabbit bank. The half-dozen boards nailed askew for a lookout in the pine tree from whose top you could sometimes see Provincetown. The dusty seedhouse with the rotting shelves and broken chairs, too far away from the house to hear a grown-up calling.

Drawn into his boyhood there, they fished in the pond, thick with closed lily pads, and spent hours in the old nursery garden on the hill, pulling the choking vines away from the bushes and plants that had survived the many years of neglect, tearing the dry grass from the wilderness of the herb plot, until the pattern of brick edges and paths began to reappear.

'When we live here,' Laurie said, 'we'll bring this garden back again. We'll get back the barn and have our own cows. Clear the pond and stock it. Make over the tennis court. We could bring the place back to what it was, and our kids will do all the things I did.'

33

When the roadway was hacked out across the parkland, across the dirt track that wandered in from the road to the barn and then on to the house, there was no way to get the cows to pasture on the other side. So the engineers had made a tunnel through the embankment, slightly higher and broader than a cow.

Laurie and Jess went through to clean out the bottles and litter that the teenagers left in summer, sneaking in at the barn end which was on the town side.

Standing in the middle of the tunnel, with her shoulders hunched against the corrugated roof to see if she could feel the cars, Jess was suddenly so perfectly happy that she said: 'I'd like to have a baby,' and they ran crouched through the tunnel together, shrieking at the echo, stumbling out through the bushes into the sun.

If this place were theirs, even the road, even the noisome, insolent road, could not spoil their life. When they kissed Sybil goodbye, they asked her, asking Melia too, for she was part of the friendliness and warmth: 'Can we come next Friday?'

4

THE CATS HAD long ago all come back to the house, to cry round Melia at the chopping board, and take swats at Tiger's rat tail, which was why he spent most of his time in the basket, looking out at them with bulging sticky eyes.

Having discovered the mice while Sybil was in the hospital, the cats often went back to the barn by way of the tunnel under the road, coming and going like subway commuters under the whining snow tyres of the sparse winter traffic. But Tiger was too stupid to learn about the tunnel. Mousing was his only blood sport, and when he wanted to visit the barn, he followed his eyes instead of his senses, and went under the fence and across the road, hoppity on three legs if it was a particularly nervous day.

When the doorknocker pounded one Saturday morning, it did not sound like doom. It sounded like the newspaper boy wanting his money.

Sybil went to the back door, which was the one everyone used, since the front door was at the opposite end of the house from the new driveway that was made when the road was built. She opened the door looking down, for the newspaper boy this year was very small, and looked straight at the dead body of Tiger, bloody in the arms of a man who said: 'I couldn't do nothing about it, lady. He run right out. It wasn't my fault. There wasn't nothing I could—'

'Nobody is blaming you,' Sybil said tartly, marvelling at her calm, but Melia pushed past her with a shriek to get to the dog, and the wake was on.

She did not cry. Sybil would have liked to comfort her, and share her grief, but Melia would not even let her talk about it.

Tight-lipped, she wrapped the dog in Sybil's new red white and blue roller towel, and laid him in the hooded basket, and took it up to her room.

She came down wearing her brown coat with the teddy bear collar, and without a word, took the car keys off the hook at the back of the cellar door.

Gone for some black crepe, perhaps. Sybil wandered about, unable to settle, ashamed of herself for wondering what was for lunch, feeling the loss, for Melia had no husband (if she had ever had one), no children, no friends or family who took any notice of her.

Only me. This is her home. I will be extra kind to her. Get her another dog. Montgomery will find another one like that.

When Melia came back with a longish parcel under her arm (crucifix? tombstone?), Sybil said kindly: 'Don't bother about cooking lunch. I don't feel very hungry today.' Which was just as well, for Melia stayed shut up in her room all day and all night, and did not answer any of the times that Sybil called anxiously through the door.

THAT FIRST TIME that Melia Mulligan got drunk, Sybil told no one. It was not Melia's fault. It was because of the dog. Anyone might get drunk if they lost a child. Even Theo, with his hard head, had got a little tipsy when his brother's boy went down in the *Astoria*, and told Sybil that he had liked his nephew better than any of his own children.

She could not tell anyone, because she was afraid they would fire Melia and put her in a nursing home, or the Old People's Housing Project. Senior citizens. On the edge of the town, half a mile from the shops, two lines of dun coloured cabins created by the Town Fathers, whose dream of dear old ladies nodding feebly to each other from their doorsteps had materialised into a collection of rather masterful old persons with all their faculties, and a perpetual feud on with their neighbours.

John? Impossible. Thelma—ha, ha. New Jersey with Mary, in that half a house, with the sullen girl roomers up top. An apartment with Laurie and Jess. But she did not want to live in an apartment. And they would not want her. The girl—the girl was all right. She was not admitting yet that she liked Jess. Might even say: I love you, if the girl would only say it first. They would be close, as long as they were apart. Sybil as a liability would finish it. The British had no mercy.

With Laurie alone, it could have worked. They had even talked of it, before he went to London. She could have looked after him. . . . Idiot, what are you saying? You can't even look after yourself. Silly old senior citizen.

While Melia was up in her room all those hours, out for the count, Sybil had found out the truth. They were right. She could not manage alone. The accident, the

37

pneumonia, the long weeks in hospital had taken some-thing from her.

Her memory had been tricky for years. That happened much earlier than people thought, but at fifty, you could pass it off as absent-mindedness. Later, she began to for-get things that had happened five or ten years before, remembering in crystal detail events like Ted's disastrous wedding, fifty years ago.

She could still remember much of the past, filed away when her brain was young and athletic; but now there were things, not only of five or ten years ago that she could not remember, but five or ten minutes.

She would find herself in a room without knowing what she had come to fetch. She had to ask Melia: Where's my cane? half a dozen times day. Once when she was tired, she forgot she had had supper.

She still tired easily. Her leg, 'good as new,' according to the surgeon, though Montgomery was never so vision-ary, still gave her a lot of pain. Shall I ever walk to the top of the hill again and see the woods and ponds and the waiting sea?

In the four years since Theo died, she had lived by her-self. How can you stay alone in this spooky old house all night? Anna used to say, slapping her great hand over her mouth as she heard the wind making oboe music in a drainpipe, or a sharp crack of old boards in changing weather. But Sybil had never been afraid of anything. Now, to her disgust, she was sometimes fearful. What of? She did not know. Melia never took a day off, since she had nowhere to go and did not fancy Boston, but if she went out to the shops or the post office after dark, it always seemed as if she was gone longer than necessary. Sybil would turn on all the lamps in the downstairs rooms, and

Melia would roll the car carefully down the drive to a house 'All lit up like Christmas!' and Sybil lied: 'I thought it would look cheerful for you.'

Cooks had come and gone at Camden House, and in the many gaps between them, Sybil had cooked for everyone, and since the war always for Theo and whoever else was there.

Her cakes had been her triumph. Even when there was a cook, it was 'one of Sybil's cakes' that honoured each anniversary, each special guest. In the doldrums of Saturday afternoon, when Melia and the mangled dog were immured above, she wanted to make a cake. There were no packets of cake mix in the cupboards, for Melia was not that sort of woman. Nor was Sybil, but when she went to the buckled, grease-spattered cook book, she could not follow the instructions.

Her brain tottered, defeated, and would not make the effort to regiment the ingredients and tell her how to start.

She could not make a cake! She, Sybil Camden Prince, feeder of a family, who had made a cake at least every three days when the children were at home.

That is how she thought of herself, fortyish, as she was in the twenties, those comfortable years when Nancy and Walter took care of what she and Theo did not want to do, but didn't act funny about what they did want to do, like Anna Romiza if you tried to help by polishing silver. 'I destroyed myself over that flatware only last week.'

She was plump at forty—where had all that flesh gone to?—pottering endlessly in the kitchen, pickling, preserving, the children knowing where to find her, knowing there was always something in the oven. She saw herself

39

like that still. Even though you knew you were eighty, addressed yourself as Old Fool, and told people: I'm only a useless old woman, you did not completely believe it. If you did, you would not wait for death to catch you. You would go to meet it.

So when Melia was locked in the room over the porch, Sybil felt fortyish and wanted to bake a cake, and when she could not, she cried, and could not understand what was wrong. She had always had a hand with cakes. Always something in the oven.

'The children never used to ask: Where's Mother?' she told Melia next day. 'They just came straight to the kitchen.'

Melia had a hangover and was not speaking. She had made a sketchy stab at a late lunch for both of them, and because she did not seem able to carry a tray into the dining room, Sybil sat down at the kitchen table and said: 'I'll have it here with you.'

The bars were down. Now that it was done, it was a great relief. She would not have to fix her hair before supper and change her slippers for shoes. She and Melia could eat fried chicken in their fingers together, and hurl the bones at the garbage pail, as she had done in the days before My Accident, when Anna had gone home and she was peacefully alone.

'We had a couple then, you see,' she chatted on to Melia, because she did not want the two of them to sit there masticating in silence, like an institution. 'Nancy and Walter. Great big people, muscles, both of them. Nancy could turn over that big mattress of mine, flip, just like that. He was in charge of the farm and the nursery, and I'll bet you never saw such peony blooms as that man raised. For Harvard Commencement, it was never any-

40

thing but peonies from Camden Gardens. Red blooms as big as your head.'

Melia laid hers in the flat of one hand, and sighed, pushing potato about with a fork.

'Peonies were always one of our specialties. I think I've told you. It's the soil. When my husband started the gardens again after World War One, some of his red peonies were plants my father had put in, before the turn of the century. The lazy man's flower he called them, because they hate to be moved.

'There was nothing he didn't know about flowers and trees, Melia, nothing. The gardens he made here— nothing like it had been seen in New England. He used to go all over the State, lecturing. I wish you could see his notebooks. I have them somewhere, with all his herbal remedies, handed down from the first settlers and the Indians. It was an old Indian helped my father lay out the gardens when he first built this house. Long before I was born, of course.'

Sybil smiled, and gave a small laugh as well, because if Melia was not looking, she might be listening, and if she was not listening, she might be looking, in spite of the aspic glazing of her eye.

Since she seemed to be doing neither, Sybil stood up and said brightly: 'I'll clear the plates.'

There was some meat on Melia's plate. As Sybil slid it away from between her disconsolate elbows, she suddenly threw back her head and howled: 'He could have had that!' and flung her whole torso down on the table with her arms outstretched, and sobbed the starch out of the chequered tablecloth.

41

After the benison of tears, the house purred on as before. Melia reverted to the treasure she had always been, the trash men took away the bottles Sybil found feebly camouflaged in the linen closet, and nothing was said.

One evening shortly before Christmas, Laurie called to ask if they could come for the weekend.

'Ask Melia to make one of her pot roasts. Mont is coming over, and we'll bring some wine.'

Wine! Sybil's thin grey hair stood on end. The word was a sluice gate opening, and memory rushed in.

Ever since Melia had come stumping in out of the light snow this morning, Sybil had been worrying where she had seen a parcel that size and shape before.

'Melia dear, where are you?'

'Hullo dear.'

That was the way they talked to each other now, like pigeons on a ledge.

Sybil went to the foot of the stairs and looked up at Melia's cheerful face, hanging over the rail above. 'Laurie and Jess are coming tomorrow. Could you make a pot roast?'

'Yes dear.'

Something had got to be said. For your sake, Melia Mulligan, I've got to brave it out now, because if they find out, you and I are goners both.

'And Melia.'

'Yes dear.'

'I don't care to say this, but you—you've got some liquor in your room, haven't you?'

Melia's pink smile disappeared. Her face closed up.

'Haven't you?'

Melia took her pudgy pastry hands off the rail. She was flushed, but steady.

42

'All I ask is this,' Sybil said, looking not up, but straight ahead at the photograph of President Harding arriving at Buzzard's Bay station on his campaign tour, 'please don't —don't make yourself sick while the children are here. Please.'

I'm not criticising, she wanted to say. I'm sure you have your troubles. We all do. I'm just lucky that mine don't take me to the bottle.

But Melia had gone to her room and shot the bolt, and was seen no more that evening. Good thing they had had supper. Or had they? Sybil was too upset to remember.

Next morning, Melia did not wake Sybil with hot chocolate, and was not cosily downstairs in her woolly breakfast slippers when she went down to investigate. Sybil climbed upstairs again, slowly, two feet on each step. Her leg was bad today. It was still snowing. Melia would never get the car up the steep driveway to get the meat. Everything was horrible.

'Melia dear.' The door was still bolted. 'Are you all right?' What was she doing? What did people do when they locked themselves in for an orgy?

The bed creaked, and Melia called out thickly: 'Go away.'

'I *asked* you!' Sybil threw away the pigeon talk, and blazed. Oh, it was too bad. Too bad of her after everything Sybil had done. 'How could you, Melia, how could you let me down like this?'

'You shouldn't have said such a terrible thing last night. You shouldn't have said that to me. You hurt my feelings.'

'So it's my fault now? Very funny,' Sybil said bitterly. 'Very, very funny.' She made a witch's face at the door, and then very slowly, like a pallbearer, went downstairs to see what must be done.

43

Laurie and Jess left the car at the top of the drive and ran down, sliding and plunging in the deep snow, ending up together with a crash against the back door, the basket swinging.

They pushed in, laughing, shaking snow, stamping their feet, clinging for a moment to press icy faces together in the little hall.

No Melia in the kitchen, no smell of meat or vegetables. They put down the small basket and went hallooing through the house. It was to be the big surprise. A puppy for Melia, an embryo creature, naked and shivering, which would grow up to be every bit as unattractive as Tiger, now buried with a wooden cross under the mountain laurel.

Sybil was upstairs, putting sheets on their bed, panting slightly, her lips a little blue.

'Where's the widow Mulligan!'

'She's lying down,' Sybil whispered, and made a mouth for them to do the same. 'She's not well.'

'What's the matter? We'll have Mont look at her,' Laurie said.

'It's nothing. She wants to be left in peace. Let's go down. We don't want to wake her.'

'But she's never sick,' Laurie objected.

'Well, she is now,' his grandmother answered sharply. 'Stop arguing and go downstairs.'

She had not ordered them about for so long that they were glad, and forgot how strained she looked in the excitement of showing her the puppy, feeding it, and chasing it with a scatter of rugs through the rooms which led into each other round the central chimney.

'What's this?' Mont said, when he arrived, whistling sweetly outside the window, like Sybil's lover. 'You look terrible, Mrs P.'

'I've had a cold.'

'You haven't.'

'Well, I'm tired. I've been wrapping Christmas presents.' He reached for her wrist, but she pulled it away. 'Leave me alone, Montgomery. When I want a physical examination, I'll tell you. You are invited to dinner, nothing more. And don't raise your eyebrows at Jess. She thinks you are too brash for a doctor too.'

'Gramma I—' She had wanted to come, but if Sybil was going to play at acid old lady, Jess would rather go back to Cambridge.

'What's for dinner?' Mont asked briskly, as if he had just come in at the door and no one had yet said anything. He asked it in his rubbing hands voice, bustling Well, well, well! into a sickroom to flatten the aching body even farther into the mattress by the exuberance of his rangy youth. Jess had seen him in action when Sybil was ill. She was not going to let him deliver her baby, whatever Laurie said. No argument yet. First she had to get pregnant.

'We were going to have pot roast,' Sybil said, 'but then Melia took sick, so I called Arthur Davis and he sent me up a nice piece of steak with his boy. I thought Jess could—'

'How long has Melia been sick then?'

'Oh—since yesterday.'

'Has Anna been here? Who's been taking care of you?'

'Don't fuss, boy. I took care of myself for years before I gave a home to Melia Mulligan.'

Jess found a small chicken pie in the stove, thawed but uncooked. Sybil must have forgotten to light the oven. She found several cats crying for food. Two were shut in the cellar, and one was in the little back bedroom off the kitchen, where it had torn up some sponge rubber curlers left behind by one of Laurie's cousins. She found a blackened milk saucepan, and a cigarette which had dropped out of an ashtray and burned a little furrow in the counter.

What if Melia were really ill? What on earth would they do!

After the steak and wine, Sybil looked so much better that someone asked her: 'What else have you eaten today?'

'Breakfast. Lunch. The usual things.'

'That chicken pie must have tasted good, stone cold with raw pastry,' Jess said. Sybil remembered, and flagged her a look which asked: Don't give me away.

Peaceful old age. What a cheat. It was even more of a battle to keep your end up than when you were young. For the first time since she had come nervously into the unknown kitchen the day before her wedding, and seen at once that she was taking Laurie not from his mother, but his grandmother, Jess felt a rush of love and pity. She put out a hand across the table, and the old woman took it, turning the gold ring on Jess's blunt finger.

'You bite your nails,' she said gruffly, but something had been achieved between them.

SYBIL WAS IN bed, and Laurie and Mont were grunting over the chessboard like pensioners. Montgomery was winning. 'Take the phone off the hook.' December was always a big month for Plymouth babies, because the

46

opening of the tourist season made April high with sap and hope.

When Jess went towards the stairs, Laurie looked up and asked: 'Where are you going?'

These days, he was very conscious of where she was, all the time. At the flat, if she went down to get the mail without telling him, he would ask anxiously: 'Where have you been?' When she went out to buy food in the late afternoon after work, they would come together again among the grocery bags and ginger ale cartons as if they had been parted by a war. It was marvellous.

'I'll be down.'

Sybil's door was ajar, to get the light from the hall. Jess shut it softly, for Sybil woke with the immediacy of age, and would want to come into Emerson's room with her. Jess wanted just to stand there by herself, and listen, and know that she was not afraid.

And she was not. Outside the window, the snow was still falling, piling softly on the bare branches, mounding over the bushes like kitchen towels spread out to dry on the gooseberries in her mother's back garden. A snow plough went by with a noise like a train, lights flashing, and a few cars, which showed the snow in the cone of their lights, before they were gone and it was falling into blackness.

Jess had left the door ajar, and she did not turn on the light. She sat on the bed, then lay down and swung up her feet. She was wearing red tights, and after she kicked her boots off when they arrived, she had not bothered to put on shoes. She hardly ever wore shoes in the house. Without them, she was just a little shorter than Laurie.

Woodwork in the room ticked. A radiator rumbled like intestines. Downstairs, Mont laughed, and a chair scraped back, and she heard Laurie at the kitchen sink, banging ice out of the tray.

Because she felt contented and secure, she shut her eyes and let herself remember that night six months ago when she had lain listening to the cars, and staring wideawake at her dismay. It had seemed such an adventure. To get Laurie's desperate cable. To plan everything in a rush. To fly to America to be married the next day. What girl she knew had ever had anything half as exciting happen to her? To be free suddenly. Flying to freedom, she had thought, with drama, peering through the plane window to see the listlessly waving figures on the roof in the rain.

And then the reckoning. She had flown, but from one trap into another. She had committed herself to a stranger, and there was no way out. She had somehow slept at last, and when she woke in a panic of fear, she had thought for an instant it was the same panic of her thoughts, before she realised that there was someone sharing the dark with her. There was someone beside her in the bed.

That was when she had screamed, and they came in and turned on the light and there was no one there. Nothing but her own sobbing breath, shuddering in her throat.

In England, Jess had never thought about ghosts. Well, there had never been any. In the kind of houses and flats her family and friends lived in, the only spectre was the landlord or the man collecting payments on the washing machine. In the stately homes she had visited with Rodge, before Laurie upset all her ideas about men: 'This is where the ghost walks,' the guide would say, but no one believed it. Most of them weren't listening. They were speculating how much things were worth, and whether the guide was a poor relation of the Duke.

You're daft, her mother would say if she could see her

48

lying on one side of the bed, with her hands by her sides and her red toes turned up like a tomb. What in the world are you lying there for in the dark with all your clothes on?

To prove something to myself.

Prove yourself to others first. What will people say?

Jess laughed, because it was funny when it was three thousand miles away, and even rather dear. From the end of the narrow passage which ran behind her head, as if in answer, came a disjointed cackle, and a small hollow sound like a ping-pong ball.

Melia's door was bolted on the inside. She would not open it, or even answer, so Laurie slid a thin file past the edge of the door, which did not fit any better than the others in the house, and edged the bolt back.

The bed was neatly made, the ornaments stood pat, the braided rugs were geometrically in place. Melia sat upright on a straight chair in the middle of the floor and recognised nobody. At her feet, the bottles of California red were ranged like candlepins. The only thing out of order was a pink plastic tooth mug which had fallen upside down on the floor, seeping a small stain.

'A wino.' Mont helped Laurie to heave her onto the bed and cover her.

'Darling Melia,' Laurie said. 'She was so perfect. Damn her.'

Woken by the noise, Sybil stood silently in the doorway with her teeth out and a stringy shawl clutched round her like a derelict.

'Don't cry, Gramma,' Jess said, as she took her arm to turn her away, and saw that her eyes were dim with tears.

'It was the toothmug. A plastic toothmug. She could have taken any of my good glasses. She knew that.'

In bed, she turned up the yellowish whites of her eyes

at Jess. 'Please don't make her go.' But she was too weak next morning to lie, and when they made her tell them that Melia had done this before, it was pack and out, with the teddy coat and the furry mittens like paws, which Sybil had given her.

Too big a risk, they said, and Sybil should have been pleased that they cared so much, but she was not. She wasn't afraid of Melia. Laurie was. He was afraid to be alone in a car with her. She might talk, or she might not, but he would not know what to say either way. Montgomery took her to a brother they discovered in Brockton, who received her without surprise, although Melia had never even mentioned him.

She took the hooded basket, and the puppy Tiger Two, 'as a memento of the happiest days of my life,' she said, and totally unmanned Montgomery in Brockton by pressing her pink velvet lips to his cheek.

Jess sent off her advertisement again to all the papers, in case of a flock of kindly widows going bust over Christmas, but without much hope. Laurie wrote to his mother and his Uncle John, but with even less hope. To both of them, since Sybil was not destitute, there was no problem.

What were they going to do? They talked it back and forth for hours, as they would later discuss their children. In bed. While they were dressing. In the kitchen while Jess was cooking and Laurie pacing the pocked black and white linoleum. Out in the snow, dragging his old sled up the hill before they came shrieking down into the big drift by the fence.

Laurie's vacation had already started, so they stayed, 'to give the old lady a good Christmas at least.' They looked on it as her last, since it seemed that she would have to leave Camden House, and nothing then would be the same again.

Sybil pottered, laying the table backwards and filling pepper mills with salt. She seemed to think that Melia was coming back. When she's better, she told visitors, even Montgomery, as if the myth of illness had never been exploded.

In the attic, Laurie found strings of coloured lights, unused since his grandfather could no longer climb ladders to decorate the house. He strung them round the gutters and gables, and decked the Norway spruce like a giant Christmas tree, staining the snow below it with light.

'Give em a treat on their way to the Cape. Next year,' Laurie said, forgetting, or pretending, 'let's floodlight the house.'

'If she can't live here, will they make her sell this place?' Jess asked.

'Would you mind?'

'I know how much you would.'

'But *you*.'

'I wouldn't have, at first. I didn't like it. I don't like you having more than me.' Jess risked honesty, because she knew he could stand her faults, and because she was going to add: 'But you know how it's grown on me. I thought it would keep us apart, this place, and your grandmother. But they've drawn us closer, haven't they?'

'Merry Christmas,' Laurie said.

'About time. I used to dread it at home. My brothers, they've married awful women. They'd stuff, and then get into a fight, and the kids were sick into paper hats.'

LAURIE HAD PLENTY of friends around Plymouth, and over the Christmas days they had parties and people in for drinks and meals, and boys came whom Sybil had not seen for years, and girls who had been children only a minute ago it seemed, now with young husbands who were clumsily charming to her.

She forgot to be tired, and her leg hardly bothered her in the excitement of having the place full of young people again, with all the fires blazing and the ice-box filled, and Jess and the other girls giggling in the kitchen, handmaids to a perpetual feast.

It would seem very quiet when it was just her and Melia again, with the cut up fryers and the knitting and the regular television programmes which accented their day. But of course, Melia was not coming back. They thought she had forgotten that, but most of the time she had not. She did not want to talk about it, or think any more about things like senior citizen housing. So she pretended that Melia would be coming back after Christmas.

On Christmas evening, when Laurie and Jess had gone to see friends, Sybil was messing about with the dishes in the sink, so that Jess would be pleased when she came home from the cocktail party.

The lights of their car came round the bend of the driveway and across the back window sooner than she expected, and she broke a cup, agitated, wanting to be done before they came in.

When the knocker of the back door thumped, she stood frozen, with her mouth open, the handle of the cup still on her finger.

Keep quiet and they will go away. Old ladies did not answer the door these days, unless they wanted to get their brains bashed in.

The knocker fell again. Montgomery always whistled, and the young people usually shoved right in, clamouring like seagulls.

'Who is it?' she called uncertainly, wishing the bolt was across, but the voice which answered was so cheery that Sybil went to the door, still holding the cup handle.

Outside on the stone mill wheel doorstep stood a short-ish, stoutish lady in high red shiny boots and a topheavy hat of some harsh grey fur like kangaroo hide. Beneath it was a fair amount of dead black hair which would fool nobody, for she was sixty-five if a day, and a brightly lip-sticked smile pushing up cheeks that were coloured high with broken veins.

All this Sybil saw with great clarity, which was unusual, for since My Accident, she was usually a little flustered meeting new people, and did not register them in detail until later.

'You'll think I have the devil's own cheek,' said the lady, putting a boot confidently on the doorstep, 'but the truth of it is this. I was driving by on the other side of the road and saw your house with all the pretty lights. The

53

first sign of cheer since I left the Canal. Such a picture in the snow, it looked, I just had to turn off and find my way across the road to tell you.'

'Why, how nice. Do come in.' Sybil stepped aside and the visitor came in, scented rather strongly, but not unpleasantly.

'Aren't I absurd?' she said. 'I've never simply obeyed an impulse like that. I don't know why I did.'

'I'm glad you did,' Sybil said, and meant it. Although Laurie and Jess were only just down the road, she had been getting a little jumpy at the sink, undecided whether it was worse to draw the curtains and not know what was outside, or to risk the pale turnip face of a Peeping Tom pressed suddenly against the black glass. 'My grandson will be back any minute, and you must stay and tell him, because he was the one put up the lights. Although it was my husband, of course, who bought them, several years ago before he died.'

'I'll introduce myself. I'm Dorothy Grue. I've been spending Christmas with my sister in Provincetown, but it's a small house, and her husband—well, one doesn't want to outstay one's welcome.' If Sybil could tell life histories before they were even into the kitchen, so could she.

'I am Sybil Prince.' She put out her hand, saw the cup handle, and they both laughed.

'I'm very glad to know you.' Miss—Mrs? (no ring) Grue put her feet apart and bent from her broad hips, knees out and forward, to pick up the broken china. Yes, she was no chicken. Only her hairdresser knew for sure. But Sybil knew. That colour at that age.

She had for some years been surprised to find how spiteful one became as one grew older. In her prime, tinted

54

hair would have been a matter of interest, perhaps admiration, if it suited the face below. But not a thing to crow over, and project a vision of herself asking Jess: Did you note the hair?

This was the first time since her illness that she had had a visitor without Melia or the children there to officiate, so she extended herself in hospitality. She hung Miss/ Mrs Grue's coat up herself on a broad wooden hanger, not a mere wire one from the cleaners, and took her into the long living room at the front of the house, not the cosier room at the back hall from the kitchen, where most of the living of the house was done.

She brought the sherry and cigarettes, and some crackers, making so many small journeys back and forth that her visitor said; 'You shouldn't put yourself out for me.'

'I'm glad to do it. I'm not allowed to do much.' She laughed. 'They think I'm helpless, since my accident.'

'Oh yes?'

When she took off her coat, it had been revealed that Dorothy Grue had an enormous shelf of pouter pigeon chest. Cardigan buttons ran down the font of it in a grand curve, over which she nodded and smiled most genially, shaking her Christmas bell earrings as she invited: 'Do tell me about it.'

IT WAS ALL settled. By the time Laurie and Jess came back, a little silly from the party, it was all settled.

Warmed by the sympathetic interest of the kindly stranger who sipped her sherry with her elbow held far out to reach past the bosom, and chain smoked with genteel compulsion, Sybil told about Melia. Not all of it. One had one's loyalties. Melia had been an angel and she would have her back tomorrow, wino or no wino, if they would let her. But enough to set the scene.

Lulled by sympathetic wags of the marsupial hat, Sybil confessed that she could no longer manage on her own, and that her future was in jeopardy.

'No housekeepers? It sounds like a very fine offer. One I would jump at, at any rate, and not shed a tear for the retail trade. When you've worked all your life to keep yourself, as I have' (Miss Grue then; bad luck not to get a husband to change your name, if nothing else), 'you begin to wonder what it's all about.'

Hold your horses, Theo used to say, to her crazy, unpractical notions, like taking all the children to Canada for the weekend. When Sybil was a child, her father called her Musket Camden, because she was always shooting off. Musket shot off now with all the old rashness. Had not Miss Grue proved herself a fellow Musket by suddenly swinging her car off the highway to go calling on a stranger?

'Come and live here then.'

'Oh, come now, I—'

'They're going to make me leave the house, I know they are.' Sybil leaned forward, knowing she was gabbling too much (it was the sherry), hearing in her voice the gossipy hiss she hated, but was too old to control, like the

56

mean triumph over Dorothy's hair. Dorothy? Hold your horses, Syb.

'I'm not saying I wouldn't be tempted. I'm not saying that at all. I wonder. . . .' She chuckled and slapped her thick thigh. 'It would make my sister sit up though. Our place on the Cape, they call it. A few boards knocked together by a carpenter's apprentice. You push a thumb tack in to hang a calendar, and the house practically falls down. But this house.' She nodded round the long room, pursing her lips at the dark family portraits, the deep faded sofa, the carved panelling in the alcove where John Camden's cumbersome desk still stood, because no one had ever been able to move it. 'If I lived in this house, know what I'd do?'

'What would you do?' They had turned in their chairs to sit facing each other, bony knees almost touching cushiony ones, Sybil's skirt drawn too far back in her eagerness, her eyes fixed on Miss Grue's eyes, which were prominent, with shiny whites like hard-boiled eggs.

'Make new curtains for that big window, for one thing. Velvet. Something rich. Wax up these old floors.'

Anna would be furious.

'Recover the chairs, if you like. I'm good at that kind of thing. I like to keep busy.'

'Oh, so do I.' Sybil was fortyish, bustling, domestic. 'We could work together. Every hour that fleets so slowly has its task to do or bear. Luminous is the crown, and holy, when each gem is set with care. Adelaide A. Proctor. I'd forgotten I remembered that. Funny how the real poetry goes, and the old trash stays with you.'

'I'm a push-over for verse too.' Miss Grue said, and sighted her eye at the sherry decanter, so that their pact might be sealed in wine.

And so when Laurie and Jess came back home, with another equally silly couple, who stopped off in the kitchen to see what they could find to cook, the fait accompli of Dorothy was presented.

All the things that Sybil had feared they would say, they did not, but Dorothy answered some of them anyway. She spoke of references. Of past jobs and family connections. Of her nephew who was Chief of Police in some town in Rhode Island.

They liked her. Sybil could see that they did, although they were not saying much that was sensible. She liked them too. She laughed good naturedly when Laurie tripped over the corner of a rug. And when Jess said: 'You shouldn't have had that last martini, darling,' and Laurie suddenly blazed: 'Cut it out—what's the matter with you?' she laughed again. But it occurred to Sybil that she had never heard him speak like that to Jess. Or to anyone.

5

'Is THAT REALLY her name?' Montgomery whispered.

Dorothy heard. Would she hold it against him? But she said brightly: 'Grue by name and grue by nature,' which did not mean a thing, although she said it as if it did.

She had quite a gift for making meaningless remarks sound significant. Even the little common exhortations, like Here we are and There you go, with which she boosted Sybil through the ploys of the day, acquired new depth. When, being one of those people who talk only medicine to doctors, she told Montgomery that she was never sick nor sorry, her heavy voice, harsh with cigarettes, made it almost a warning, or a threat. No more big meat and gravy meals? Poor Montgomery had better start looking for a wife again.

'I'll stop by in a couple of days to check that lung.' He put his long, strong hand on Sybil's shoulder, and she reached up and patted it. She was very fond of him, and believed that he had saved her life, although at the time, if she remembered right, it had seemed easier to die.

'No need to worry about *her*,' Dorothy said cheerfully. 'She's in good hands now, you know.'

'Mrs Mulligan was nice enough,' Montgomery said mildly, but Dorothy capped him.

'An alcoholic.' She had been a practical nurse in the days before they were called that, and had as little use for doctors as a Christian Scientist.

'I'll stop by in a day or so,' Montgomery repeated, for it would take more than a nurse to put him off. He was the only doctor at the hospital who had no dread of the charge nurse in Obstetrics. 'But thanks for taking such good care of her.'

Bless you, Sybil thought, for being nice to her. Dorothy was her discovery, and she wanted everyone to like her and be pleased that she was there in the side room over the porch, with yet another new spread, because Melia's had to be burned. The poor woman had led quite a sad kind of life, what with one thing and another, and her fiancé being killed, and there being nothing to sit on behind the ground floor counters at Merricks, to whom she had given her best years and her arches, industrious fool that she was.

On his first visit after Dorothy moved in, with enough baggage for a siege, Laurie had said: 'Don't let her treat you like a child,' because Dorothy had been a little assertive about vegetables. But she would grow on him, just as she was growing on Sybil, with her energy and her loves and hates—nothing in between for anybody—and her decisions made like a knife, swift and clean so that Sybil had no worries.

Melia Mulligan had been a lovely woman, but she had

always been consciously a servant, expecting orders, paid to keep her lady comfortable and content. Dorothy Grue was a friend. Someone who shared the house and just happened to do most of the work because she was the strongest. She took no orders. If you wanted something done, you had to say: 'We'll have to think about cleaning out the spice rack,' or: 'I think I'll change my sheets today,' and Dorothy would chip in at once: 'Thinking never got anything done. It's on my list for this morning.'

At the beginning of the month, although the cheque-book would be lying handily on Sybil's desk among the welter of clippings, old letters and indecipherable memos to herself, there was no direct transaction. Sybil had to leave the cheque in a stamped envelope on the table in the hall, and on her next trip to the post office, Dorothy would mail it to herself, and collect it the following day from their box. Heaven knew what Frances and Bea thought, for they had been at the post office for years and knew Sybil's writing, but there it was. There were these niceties about Dorothy, and they would never chew drumsticks together within range of the garbage can; but Sybil could accept prim dining-room meals with the appliqué cloth which cost seventy-five cents to launder, and the pretence that Dorothy drank prune juice because she liked the taste.

It was worth it.

Melia had been a delightful accessory, but Dorothy was a whole outfit. She brought to the house a feeling of life and activity which Sybil, waning, craved. The young people brought a sense of beginnings. Dorothy brought a sense of something accomplished. In the evening, as they sat with their ritual sherry, she would swat her rubbery thigh and say: 'Well, we've had quite a day of it!' And even though Sybil had done almost nothing, she would feel she had been busy all day.

To understand Dorothy, as Sybil pointed out to Laurie and Jess, you had to understand about Roger. He was the most important thing in her life, her lover and her child, and if anything should happen to him, it would be worse than Melia with Tiger.

Roger Grue was a budgerigar, a male of brilliant oily green and yellow plumage. He lived in a vast domed cage like the concourse of Pennsylvania Station, hanging high in the kitchen above the cats, who sat in a Druids' ring below, convinced that they could hypnotise him.

One of Dorothy's first acts of self assertion, after she had finished praising everything in sight, including the Priscilla stove on which she threatened to cook, had been a sweeping: 'The cats will have to go.'

Sybil refused. Whose house is it? her mind prompted her, as if there were some danger of forgetting. She had always had cats, even when her mother was alive, and allergic—only it was called nerves in those days. Even when she and Theo were in that dreadful plum-coloured house at Amherst, where John and Thelma had scarlet fever, before the war.

When Sybil announced, with all the old vehemence she was afraid she had lost: 'The cats are staying,' she thought for a moment that Dorothy would pack. Her impressive chest went even further up and out as she drew in breath through nostrils that were cut back and blood-shot, like a racehorse.

They measured eyes, and then she let out the breath on a laugh, and the cough which always followed it. 'Anything you say. It's your house, after all.'

There you see, said Sybil to the unseen audience of critics. Nothing to worry about.

So the farmer's son Bobby, who did odd jobs for Sybil after school, fixed a hook in the ceiling near the sunniest window, too high for the cats, or for the head of anyone except Montgomery, who would not bump it twice. To reach the cage, Dorothy bought a chrome and plastic stool with a shiny red seat, which converted to a little pair of steps. It was hideous in the kitchen, where everything was old wood and wallpaper, but there it was.

When the cage door was open, the bird perched on the outside of the bars, rattling them with his beak like a boy with a stick and railings, or made clattering tours high up the wall, alighting on Dorothy's shoulders, where he could mumble her face with his Armenian beak and deride the cats with his flat unfocused eye.

Dorothy talked to him incessantly, and when he was not in a muttering narcissistic trance before the mirror in his cage, he talked back. He had dozens of phrases which he used haphazardly, reeling off twenty or so at a time, like a tape recorder. Hullo Dot. Soup and sandwich. Pardon me for living. Roger loves Mother. He had given Sybil several shocks, and would give her many more, for although one of the cats could chirrup like a bird when it was stalking, she had never had a talking bird, and it would take some getting used to.

From his gilded pleasure dome under the kitchen ceiling at Camden House, he quickly picked up several new items. Hullo Sybil. What's for lunch? Oh those cars. Bedtime, Sybil—when Dorothy took down

63

the cocoa mug which Laurie had once painted shakily: 'Grandma.'

Dorothy thought he was a genius, although most of what he said was unrelated nonsense.

'He knows everything I say,' she claimed. 'He knows what he's talking about better than some folk I could mention.'

Nonsense, Sybil wanted to say, but there was a chance that Dorothy meant her, so she let it pass.

Dorothy declared: 'That bird is all but human,' and there were times when you could almost believe it. For the uncanny thing about Roger, the unnerving thing that caught you off guard if you had forgotten him, was that he spoke in Dorothy's voice.

Everything he said was in her tone, muted a little and husky, but the huskiness was hers, the pitch and vowel sounds identical. He could even imitate her cough, and the tch-oh, with which she greeted an empty matchbox or verdigris on the pickle relish.

When he called out: 'Come on Sybil!' she often answered: 'Where to?' before she realised Dorothy was not in the room. Once, coming down the back stairs, she heard him say: 'Have a hot biscuit,' and put on a courteous smile for Dorothy's visitor. But there was no one there except two cats on duty, and the bird, and the radio playing softly to keep him company.

'You make a fool of me.' Sybil shook her stick at him, and he gave a hacking cough and told her: 'Dot loves Roger.'

He was Dorothy's familiar, her alter ego. Her doppelganger, Laurie said, but that was too sinister for the relationship that existed so cosily between the budgerigar and Dorothy Grue.

64

'Perhaps it's your fiancé,' Jess said, one Saturday at the end of March, when they were snowed in again by the late blizzard which always belied the radio voices babbling, by the calendar, of Spring. 'Perhaps Roger is a reincarnation of Henry. Most people, if they were given the chance, would come back as an animal or a bird, I should think, not as a person.'

They knew all about Henry by now. Dorothy had quite taken the young couple to her pouter pigeon bosom, and relaxed with them at weekends, as if they were part of the family. No. Sybil shook her brain as she often had to, like a watch, to make it tick properly. As if *she* were part of the family.

They knew about Henry and the car accident, and where Dorothy was when she heard the news, and how it was up to her to tell his mother. 'They called me first.' That was the crowning triumph over a woman she never had the chance to triumph over as a mother-in-law.

'Perhaps you're right dear,' Dorothy said. The bird sat on the end of her pen, as he often did when she wrote letters, making kissing noises and riding back and forth across the page. 'Henry used to write to the papers a lot. He was a mine of ideas. Perhaps Roger does guide my pen then. My friends all tell me I write a very interesting letter.'

What do you write about? Sybil sometimes wondered. What do you write them about me?

'It's probably a woman anyway.' Laurie said a little sulkily. He was moody this weekend, as Sybil had not seen him since he was in the limbo between school and college, bored with everything except this house and her. 'One day it will lay an egg.'

'If he does, it will be a biological miracle,' Dorothy

65

said brightly. She rode over moods by ignoring them. 'You can tell he's a male by the blue round his nostril, see?'

'Poor soul, that's why he's so opinionated,' Jess said. 'Why don't you get him a mate?'

'He wouldn't talk. He'd chat to her instead of me.'

'How cruel.' Jess glanced at Laurie, sprawled yawning in the splayed armchair. 'He's probably a mass of frustrations.'

Dorothy's colour had risen a little. The bird flew from the pen onto her head where it nested, beady-eyed, in the hair which was locked in the bathroom for a long session every three weeks. Sybil had found the bottle when she was poking in the trash can to see what it was the bird had broken, flying into the dresser; but she would never tell. Dorothy had never told the children, or Montgomery, or Thelma when she came last week, that Sybil had mistaken Alice Manning whom she knew quite well, for Nancy Parkes whom she knew equally well, and sent a detailed message to Alice's mother, who had been dead for twenty years. Not gossiping about Dorothy's hair was a small price to pay for saving her own face.

'Women always assume that men are frustrated without a mate. If that thing is Henry,' Laurie said, 'he's got it made. All food and no work and he does all the talking.'

Dorothy laughed, but Jess frowned and said: 'That's silly. Like a rotten magazine cartoon, as if all married men were trapped.'

Once, Sybil would have been shamefully pleased to see them almost quarrel. Not quarrel, but look at each other with cold knowledge.

Now, because she accepted Laurie as Laurie and Jess,

66

and they were her candidates for the future, it was distressing. Perhaps the girl was pregnant. But surely they would tell her?

Next day, the sun glittered on the new snow, and they played outside all morning, and when they came in starving for roast chicken, they were tangibly, almost embarrassingly, in love.

It had been an up and down weekend, all the same, and on Sunday evening Sybil dozed in her chair. Dorothy's light tap on the shoulder was a guilllotine blow which woke her with a start.

'Time for bed,' Dorothy said in Roger's voice. 'I'll bring up your hot drink.'

She went into the kitchen, and at the clink of china, the bird said: 'Bedtime, Sybil,' with the mindless response of a ventriloquist's dummy.

Sybil climbed slowly and creakily with her head down, as if the stairs were a mountain. When she reached the top and looked up, there was her mother.

She was standing in the hall, half turned away, with her arms folded into a muff in front of her. She was wearing her long brown travelling suit with the braided jacket, and the big green cavalier hat with the veil. Her face was hidden by the veil, and for the fraction of a second while her heart stopped, Sybil was overwhelmed with loss. Then her heart began to thump and bang so that she could hardly breathe, and she clung to the banister post while Dorothy came up behind her, laughing and coughing, and ripped off the veil, and the wadded newspaper fell from the wooden neck of Bella Camden's dummy.

'How do you like my joke?'

'Ha, ha,' Sybil croaked, through her hammering heart.

She would be all right if she could just get to her room and lie down.

'Just my little joke. I'm a push-over for jokes, you know.'

6

'THAT FIRST WINTER in the harbour,' Sybil told Dorothy, who knew shockingly little about Pilgrim history, although she claimed to be a push-over for the past, 'was nearly the last. Half of them died from some dreadful disease, poor souls. They started burying them up on the hill, but when more people kept dying, they flattened out the mounds and sowed a crop over, to fool the Indians.'

Dorothy raised her eyebrows, which were inked in to match her hair.

'They didn't know much about medicine, beyond things like stewing bugs in wine, so after a bit the old Indian women began to teach them their herbal remedies.'

'No Wonder Drugs in those days,' put in Dorothy, who could not listen for long without comment, even when she had nothing intelligent to say.

'That's right, Dot.' Call me Dot, she had said, and Sybil was trying, but it made her feel like the bird. Dot loves Roger. Hullo Dot, scratch a bird. 'And one of the colonists made some notes for a herbal, and that was my ancestor Will Camden. Great, great—'

'You told me.'

'And it was his grandson,' she could see him now, labouring with his own brown hands, sweating in a jerkin and breeches, 'built one of the first big houses in the town. There's a gift shop there now. They pulled it down for termites. But it was older than the Owens house, that Maud is so proud of, and better built as I remember. Mustn't it have been pretty, without all the stores and gas stations and sea-food restaurants, just those graceful white houses running down the hill to the harbour. Do you think we have been born in the wrong century?'

'No doubt of it,' Dorothy said. 'I've always seen myself as Nell Gwynne. But listen here. If we don't think our modern buildings are pretty, why should they have thought theirs were in the days when they were modern? Got you there.'

'I wasn't trying to score a point.' Dorothy often tried to turn a harmless conversation into a contest. 'I was trying to tell you about this house, since you asked.'

'Pardon me for living.' Dorothy inflated her red-hot nostrils.

'When my father married his first wife, Charity, Charity —I even forget her family name, can you beat that? I always knew everything Papa told me about our family. He built this house for her. It was yellow then and ever since. Colonial yellow. It was the dead of the country in those days. New England was sprouting factories and mills, so there was this movement to get back closer to Nature. They were all in it, people like my father and Emerson and Hawthorne and Alcott. Louisa May held me on her knee once, when I was a baby. When Papa's father wanted him to go into business, he said: I aim to raise flowers, not dollars. That's what he used to tell me. Flowers not dollars, Sybbie, there's your soul's profit. Although as it turned out, he did very well with the nursery gardens. Trees and plants from all over. Anything would grow for him. I've seen him talk to a plant as he set it in, asking it if it would be all right. That must seem silly to you.'

Dorothy shrugged. 'You're the one who said it.' She was knitting, with great needles like rolling pins and thick wool, to make a sailing sweater for Laurie. It was only when she was doing something like counting stitches or following a dressmaking pattern or a recipe, that Sybil got the chance to ramble on. It was not always that she could remember much to ramble on about. It came in fits and starts, like doors opening on a gust of wind. If it came when Dorothy was not a captive audience, Sybil would tell some of it to the bird, which was better than muttering it to herself like a crazy old woman. For it had to be given shape between the lips, like the breviary prayers of a priest.

'It was so quiet out here. He used to make me stand still and listen. You can hear things growing, he'd say. Imagine that now.'

The cars were always there at the back of everything: talk, music, the clatter of pans, everything but the television sing-along shows, which Dorothy turned up full blast and sang-along to.

'Here at the quiet limit of the world. . . . He built this house with love. And Charity loved it. Much more than my mother, his second wife, ever did. She died at the new moon, did Charity, and they say her tree would weep at nights, when the moon was new.'

'What tree?' Dorothy looked up, repoussé eyeballs glistening.

'It's gone now. They cut it down for——' Sybil stuck out

71

her tongue towards the road. 'He planted two trees, John and Charity, on either side of the driveway that used to run through the pasture from the town road. There was a board at the gate. Camden House Nurseries. The finest herb garden in New England, and he knew all the old Indian remedies, passed down from Will Camden. When he died, Ted was married and gone, and I was barely sixteen, and my mother didn't care, so it was all let go, till my husband and I moved back after the war. The first war, of course. You wouldn't remember that.' Though she would, all right, and could have been a nurse then. Sybil had to pretend she did not know how old Dorothy was, but she had sneaked a look at her driver's licence.

'When Papa died, my mother took to her room. She'd heard about Hawthorne's mother shutting herself up for forty years in the house at Salem, and vowed she'd do the same. But with her it only lasted forty hours of trays outside the door. She came down in a rage, and she and I lived here together.'

Nowhere to escape. When she was a child, running to her father—Wait for me, Papa! Her stepbrothers used to mimic her—Wait for me, Papa!

Then he died, as he had to, for he was sixty when she was born, and left her with Marma. Kisses and tantrums, and waiting on her and hiding the little grey kitten behind boxes in the cellar, sick with anxiety that she might find it. Wait for me, Papa—but he had gone, and left her a prisoner.

A sleeping Princess, Theo called her. Marma took to her room again.

'Poor Marma,' she said, with a sudden memory of the old forced loyalty. 'She wore black to my wedding.'

'My sister and I were going to start an antique shop

72

once,' Dorothy said, not so inconsequentially, for Sybil's wedding was ancient history. 'We were offered this old barn at Middleborough, only she got married.'

'The summer people will buy anything.'

'I didn't mean that.' Dorothy gathered up her ball of wool and stabbed the giant needles through it criss cross, like a regimental badge. 'I meant genuine antiques.'

Melia Mulligan had recoiled from Priscilla aghast, but one of the things Sybil liked about Dorothy was that she appreciated the fine old stove, and asked Anna to black-lead it every week. That was one of the reasons why Anna did not like Dorothy, but there were others.

The stove had been converted to burn oil some time ago, although it had not been used for years. Dorothy got in a jar of kerosene, and when the electric stove boiled the milk over or turned out a lopsided cake like a tam-o-shanter, she often threatened it that she would be glad to cook on Priscilla when the summer hurricanes knocked out the power lines.

Her passion for antiquity extended also to Emerson. 'A part of our (she pronounced it ower) literary heritage,' although it was doubtful whether she had read a line. After a while, she asked if she could move her things and sleep in the front room.

Sybil wanted to say No. Where would she go at night when she could not sleep and wanted to cast witch's spells on the cars? But by now, when Dorothy asked if she could do something, it was the same as saying she was going to do it.

But she was so kind. So dependable. Sybil closed her mind to criticism, for Dorothy was making herself indispensable. Already, in a few months, it was hard to imagine how she had managed this house without her, or even her own daily life, which Dorothy now had in such a reassuring grasp.

Sybil had not said anything about the breathing, since it did not seem Dorothy's kind of story. But she said: 'Emerson went out of his mind, you know. He told Papa that his essay on Shakespeare was written by the Holy Ghost.'

'Perhaps it was,' said Dorothy, who had nothing against the Catholic Church.

'He thought he was risen from the dead,' Sybil went on hopefully. 'He died before I was born, but at the end, they said, he looked as if he had come from the tombs, just a web of skin over a skull.'

'Your grandmother-in-law is trying to scare me,' Dorothy told Jess. 'She's wasting her time. In hospital, I was the only one who wasn't silly about the cadavers.'

'Is that your room now?'

'Why not? Best bed in the house. What's the matter, child?' Jess's pale eyebrows were half circles when she was surprised, her brown eyes wide. 'Is there something funny about that room?'

'No.' Jess let down her eyebrows. 'Oh no, of course not.' She looked at Sybil, but the old woman turned away, fiddling arthritically with the tangled spools in her sewing basket.

Dorothy had been several times to stare down at Plymouth Rock under its stone canopy. If Sybil were sitting in the car, for she would no more cross the road to look at the landing stone of her ancestors than a Londoner would look up at Big Ben to see the time, Dorothy would heckle her: 'How do they *know* it's the one?' They need not try any tricks with her. She was not your gullible tourist.

How did they know? Sybil had never thought to ask.

'How do they know what Priscilla Mullins said to John Alden?'

'They don't.' Dorothy started the engine and made a terrible noise with the gears. You could never best her in argument, but Sybil liked to try, for fear her wits would slip away from her completely.

When the Mayflower II came out of winter hibernation, Dorothy went down and inspected that, above and below decks, and drove in her humpbacked car, which had no shine left on the two-tone green paint, out to the replica of the first Pilgrim village.

'You come too, Sybilla.' That was her sweetness name. 'I'll bet you've never been. I knew a woman lived in Buffalo all her life and never saw the Falls.' Although she did not seem to have many friends or relations Dorothy knew 'a woman' to fit almost every situation.

'It's the walking,' Sybil said. But really it was the driving. She could just endure the trip into town with Dorothy, because it was better than not going at all, but farther than that took years off her life, which she could not spare.

Laurie had sold Sybil's car for her, before Dorothy could get the idea of driving it, but she was quite content with Two-tone, which she handled as if it were the last car left on the road. She drove quite slowly, 'no risks for me,' with a line of frenzied drivers behind her taking frightful risks to get past. She stalled her engine on railroad crossings and going the wrong way up busy one-way streets, and would not use the direction lights for fear of wasting the battery.

When her sister came from Provincetown, she took her to the Pilgrim settlement, and brought her back to the house afterwards. The sister, with a name like Mrs

75

Outboard—Sybil never did get it—was younger and thinner than Dorothy, with protruding teeth and the darting eye of a Welfare agent sent out to investigate an Assistance claim.

Sybil had the percolator going when they returned, and the coffee cups set out, with the cream and sugar. If Dorothy had said they wanted tea, or taken over the hospitality, it would have hurt. But why should it hurt that she thanked Sybil extravagantly and praised her, and called Mrs Outboard's attention to the pretty traycloth she had chosen?

'That lacquer tray's a nice piece,' the sister said, writhing her lips in her life's perpetual struggle to get them over her teeth. 'You've got a lot of fine old things here, Mrs Prince.'

'Why, thank you.' Sybil was pleased with her. She took her all over the house, showing her its small rarities and treasures; but after supper, when she suggested staying overnight, as it was getting late, the sister looked alarmed, and left hastily for Cape Cod.

'Did I say something wrong, Dot?'

Dorothy laughed, riding the bird on her stubby finger, wiggling the nail for him to nibble. 'She doesn't like old houses.'

'But she was so interested in seeing everything!'

'You made it rather difficult for her not to be.'

The bird began a long insane monologue about paper boy and where's the money and come on Sybil, and Dorothy began to chatter back at him. To keep herself from apologising in her own home—for something she had not done!—Sybil went away to telephone Laurie and Jess. They were out. After a while, she still knew that she felt badly, but she could not remember why.

76

Dorothy went back to the Pilgrim village again, to look at the herb gardens and talk to the lady dressed as a Settler who had an exhibit of pill-rolling and do-it-yourself medicine, which had greatly taken her fancy.

Montgomery still came to see Sybil, but he never got a meal during the week. By some coincidence, it was always the day they were having boiled eggs, or there were just two chops for dinner. He often came when Laurie and Jess were there, but that was different. Dorothy was jovial and lavish with him then, as if she thought he should stick to his doctoring all week and only be a real person on Sundays.

Her distrust of the medical profession extended to drug stores and patent medicines. She went Tshah! at the television commercials about the man who wouldn't buy his kids a puppy because he had a sour stomach, and she had a running feud with the druggist who had sold her a bottle of useless elixir when her cough threatened to strangle her, and had given her short measure on a bottle of a hundred aspirin tablets for Sybil. Dorothy had counted them and there were only ninety-eight.

But soon she would be able to thumb her nose at all such quackery. It was not that her cigarette cough was any milder or that the pin in Sybil's femur had stopped aching. But she was on to something better.

Waxing up with her usual furious energy the carved panelling in the alcove where Sybil's father used to sit and ponder cross-pollination, she had touched off the secret cupboard which Sybil had forgotten, and found John Camden's notes on herbal remedies.

'You don't mind?' Dorothy asked, after she had already had them spread out on the front room carpet all afternoon, kneeling over them like a grazing Welsh pony.

It gave Sybil quite a shock to see her father's tidy writing, the ink still very black, the footnotes precise. 'Linctus = a substance to be licked up.' 'No hist: evidence of efficacy of Shep: Purse in Haematemesis.'

Here were the notes he had prepared for his great lecture to the Rhode Island Horticultural Institute, which they had reprinted in their journal. Here were the directions for the concoction of wild parsnips and bilberries which he and Sybil had once tried on a coughing cow.

Laurie and Jess had done a lot of work in the herb garden on the hill, and saved quite a few of the plants. Many of Theo Prince's metal labels were still in place in the geometrical plots. When warmer days came, and the cars bore down more heavily each weekend to the sea, Dorothy bought gardening gloves, and a pair of shoes which looked like boxes on her short feet, and spent most of her spare time up in the famous Camden herb garden, weeding and dividing and transplanting, and settling in new plants she ordered from a nurseryman in Connecticut.

'We shall make our own remedies.'

'Like Indian women,' Sybil said.

'Like Pilgrim maids.' No one, mercifully not Anna Romiza, guessed the immensity of Dorothy's colour prejudice.

In the old wooden seed house, where Sybil's stepsisters had measured out seed for the packets in silver spoons, Dorothy scrubbed out some of the slatted drying shelves and laid about the lairs of ancient spiders with a balding corn broom.

Talking and thinking about the old times of seeds and herbs and all the land busy with sweet grass and plants and little fir trees in military rows, reminded Sybil of what was in the cellar. She remembered it when Dorothy was out-side, but she must do something about it before she forgot. Dorothy was too far off to call, and she always pretended not to hear the brass ship's bell outside the back door, since the time Sybil called her in for something vital and had forgotten it by the time she had plodded down through the cows.

The cellar stairs were steep and had no handrail. Just the steps on the other side of the door in the kitchen, going down into the middle of the earthy cellar, where brooded the great rainwater cistern, which once held all the water supply. Empty now, everyone hoped, although nobody had lifted the heavy wooden lid for years.

Impossible for Sybil, even with her cane, so she dropped a cushion on the top step, lowered herself to sit on it, and propelled herself down with her hands, like a child on a tea-tray.

When Dorothy came in, earth under her nails, sweat-ing, agricultural, Sybil was slumped at the kitchen table with a shot of brandy, under verbal fire from the bird, who liked to see people busy.

'All right there, lady?' Dorothy narrowed her eyes at the brandy. She once knew a woman who was an alcoholic, and could cap any tale about Melia.

Sybil nodded. 'Look what I found for you.' Cobwebby on the draining board, for her strength had not extended to washing them, were the pestle and mortar, the corru-gated pill board and roller, the earthenware jar and pewter pan—all Papa's old equipment with which he had tried out Will Camden's herbal lore.

'Oh clever Sybilla!' And Sybil glowed like a schoolgirl and forgot her exhaustion and her fear that she had done her heart in at last. Dorothy was always saying: You can stretch a heart just so far, and Sybil saw it like an over-taxed fiddle string, snapping—doing-g-g! and that would be the end.

She had forgotten most of what her father showed her, for she had only been a child, playing in her mother's pinafore, but it would come back. She and Dot would be Pilgrim maids together, and make simples and salves and electuaries. Idea! They would use Priscilla, said Dorothy.

Yes, they would use Priscilla. She was Marma's cooking stove. But it was not Marma, it was Papa who was so very close in the kitchen. Wait for me, Papa—The Lord created medicines out of the earth, he said, in his gentle instructive voice, and he that is wise will not abhor them.

7

FOR THE FOURTH of July holiday, the house was full again.

'We'll see,' was Dorothy's disturbing reply when Jess said: 'I hope it's not too much for you.'

What if it was? What would they see then? Someone had opened a new nursing home outside the town, low and streamlined as a luxury motel, with a few old folk out in wicker chairs on the tiny lawn, like stage props.

'That looks quite nice,' Jess said brightly, driving Sybil to the library. But the grandmother had stiffly turned her head the other way and would not look.

Laurie had brought his friend Peter, who was to crew for him in the sailboat races. Sybil's younger daughter Mary had come from Camden, collecting Uncle Ted from the New York club where he lived with several other shuffling old men who were much happier than anyone believed.

'Why can't I crew for you?' Jess asked Laurie. She had sailed with him last year, and every weekend of this summer, though she had not expected that. She had counted on being pregnant by now, but she wasn't, so why be left at home as if she was?

'Darling, I'm planning on a few wins.' He laughed and kissed her, and Peter laughed his unamused Princetonian neigh. She wished they had not brought him. He was a eunuch, not even a queer, but he liked Laurie's company without her.

They went to the boat dock and then to the beach to swim, without coming back for her. 'If I'd wanted the kind of man who went off with the boys all the time, I'd have married an Englishman,' she said.

Laurie laughed again, pulling a shirt over his head, and pushed her backwards onto the bed and fell on her, his shirt still over his face.

'Excuse *me*.' Dorothy said at the door. 'But your grand-mother wants to know who is going to meet Mr Camden and Miss Prince.'

Laurie swore, and Dorothy said: 'Tut, tut, Loll' (no one *ever* called him Loll). 'I'll have to wash your mouth out with soap.'

It was not only that she always came into rooms without knocking, or that she had a gift for intruding on people in love, in the garden, or behind a door, or wherever they happened to be. It was her attitude of innocent unconcern, as if they were children in the bath.

Jess had met Aunt Mary briefly at her wedding, a colourless, nearsighted woman, with the figure of a flat girl in the wrong kind of clothes, and fine nut-brown hair in a juvenile cut.

At the wedding, she had worn a dress like a Girl Scout uniform, but she had been the only one who did not seem to be adding Jess up and thinking: What's so special about her that Laurie wouldn't have chosen an American girl?

When Jess had rent the night with her screams and sobs, Mary had not crowded round her asking questions she could not answer. But she had said next day, when the others were commiserating with her swollen, shadowed eyes: 'She looks all right to me.'

The family knew her as poor Mary, and she had adopted the buffoon's defence of deriding herself before they could. Trust me to make a hash of it. Missed the bus again. Not me, I'll crack the camera.

Sybil was impatient with her, thumping the cane which had become so much another limb to her that it was hard to remember what she had gestured with before. Uncle Ted moved his garden chair behind a bush so that Mary could not disturb him with chatter, and Dorothy practically threw her out of the kitchen, for she would drive you mad fiddling, and asking what to do next.

Jess took her down to the yacht club to see the races, and she watched the wrong boat all the way and cried out: 'Bravo, Laurie!' when somebody else won.

It was boring. 'Do you want to swim?' But Mary had not swum since she was a girl. Her ears. The late afternoon was cooling when they got back to the house, and Mary said, with a naïve enthusiasm for anything that was something to do: 'Let's take a walk. It will stimulate my appetite.'

She ate so much already that Uncle Ted had asked her last night whether she had worms; but Jess agreed, and was surprised to find herself thinking: And Laurie will come home with Peter, wanting to tell me about the races, and he won't know where I am.

Barefoot, in shorts, with Mary in a cotton dress three seasons too long, and rimless dark glasses clipped over her powerful spectacles, they walked together amicably over the cropped turf and through the long dry patches the cows rejected to see what Dorothy had done in the garden of Mary's father and grandfather.

'That thyme will never thrive there.' Mary did not know much about horticulture, but she had an eye for what would fail.

She sat down on a tumbling low stone wall—you could never imagine her as a child, sprawling on grass—while Jess pushed a vine into place on the lattice that she and Laurie had repaired last year. Dorothy had worked, but only in the herb plot. The little bushes of potentilla, that Laurie and Jess had saved to flower again in papery yellow, were half strangled with crab grass. When this place is ours . . . But it was the first time she had been up here without Laurie, and if he didn't care, it might as well be left to Dorothy and the crab grass.

The seedhouse, leaning a little on its rotting timbers, was still very warm, although the sun was gone from the cracked windows and the skylight. There was a dusty incense of old earth in flower pots, and the leaves and roots and seeds that Dorothy had laid out to dry.

'They're going to make herbal remedies.'

'Do more harm than good, I expect,' Mary said. 'I remember once when I had a cold that went to my sinuses, the way my dumb old colds always do, Mother brewed me some kind of privet tea her father used to make, and I threw up all over the stair carpet. I was always throwing up. "Thar she blows," John used to say.'

She had been a weakly child, always ill to spoil a journey or a treat, sick with excitement before every Boston theatre trip, frantic with nightmares for three years until they found her adenoids had grown again.

She had even been afraid of the harmless, dusty seedhouse. 'Thelma locked me in here once,' she told Jess, 'and when they found me, I couldn't speak for an hour.'

'Why didn't you break a window?'

'I didn't think of it. I was such a dope. The little kids in my room at school have far more sense than I ever had.'

Jess yawned. A lassitude had been creeping over her during the day, weighing her down like coming thunder. It was the same feeling as after her rare fights with Laurie, when she almost dislocated her jaw yawning and yawning; but they had not fought today. The friction over Peter was still half a joke.

'I'm boring you,' Mary said, without surprise. 'Let's go down.'

At the bottom of the sloping pasture, they pushed through the heavy curtain of leaves and stood inside the cool secret tent of the weeping beech. The lower branches, flat and grey like the necks of the prehistoric animals that once roamed here, bent down so heavily to the earth that some of them had rooted there and risen beyond in a sea-serpent curve to bury themselves again, leaves rotting in the turf, far away from the trunk.

Mary's name was carved on the smooth bark, shaky and shallow, where the other family names were deep and bold. The day that Jess was first so happy here, they had run out of the cow tunnel to the tree, and Jess had cut her name in beside Laurie's boyhood carving, and they had marked out a box below, for the names of their children.

'I used to come here when I was a child,' Mary said, 'and sit on the branches and pretend it was a horse, because I was too scared to ride the pony. We had this maid then, Polly was her name, she'd lived all her life around here, and she used to tell me the old legends of the town about the poisoned house, and the knocking on the bricked-up doorway, and the old man who was condemned to wander till the crack of doom. The others wouldn't listen to her, but I always listened. She told me these branches had the souls of animals and would scream if you cut too far into them. That's why I—' She ran a finger over the feebly scratched letters of her name. 'You think I was as crazy as she was, I'll bet.'

'Don't you believe it now?'

'Well I—I hadn't thought. The weeping tree has gone, anyway.'

'Tell me.' If Jess had had a Polly, what would there have been to shiver about in the long afternoons of childhood? In the suburban road of cheap identical houses in narrow plots of land like piano keys, there were no skeletons to knock in coal sheds, no ancients wandering eternally in nothing but a beard.

'Charity and John. They were twin oak trees my grandfather planted on either side of the driveway when he came here with his first wife. But my grandmother Bella, his second wife, was always jealous of Charity, so after he died, she did something to the Charity tree, cut into it with an axe or something, and Polly said that ever after, it would weep at the new moon.'

'Did it?'

Mary had unclipped the dark glasses. Her eyes were small and expressionless behind the thick lenses of her spectacles. She nodded. 'I saw it.'

'*You* saw it?' This was different from hearing about Polly's tales. It was cold in the sunless temple of the tree. Above, the leaves were a rich green fountain above the oaks, but down here they never got the sun, and they were pale and still, like under water.

'I went out one night after everyone was asleep. I can't

86

think how, for I was always nervous at night. I used to pay Thelma half my allowance to let me sleep with her. Sometimes she took the money, and then locked her door. I went down to the tree. The moon was a finger nail. It was dark. I couldn't see it. I felt it. It was bleeding like a wound. But when I got indoors and looked at my hand, it was dry.'

Dorothy began to ring the ship's bell like a wild woman for Jess to come and help her, but Jess and Mary pushed out through the curtain of branches on the other side of the tree, so she would not see them, and Mary showed Jess where the Charity tree had stood, near the end of the cow tunnel.

Above, the traffic flashed through the setting sun like an endless train, the noise of each car a part of the whole. 'It must have been terrible when you found out where they were going to put the road.'

'I never really liked this place,' Mary said, 'so it wasn't so bad for me. It about killed Mother. They'd been talking about by-passing the town for years, but no one dreamed—well, who would, when there's so much scrubland all around? I remember the day, I'll never forget it. Mother was in the front room, and she suddenly screamed out. I ran in. I thought she was ill. She was standing by the window like a statue, and there were men walking through our meadow, knocking in stakes. Walking through. Just like that. They crossed the driveway and one of them put down his mallet and leaned against the Charity tree to light a cigarette. He looked towards the house and saw us watching, and he waved. Waved! I thought Mother would have a fit.'

The bell rang again, as if the place was on fire, and they turned towards the house.

87

'They didn't start the road for a long time after that. Mother used to pull up the stakes, and they'd come and knock some more in. I wasn't here when the twin oaks came down. I asked her. I wanted her to tell me there had been a scream or a thunderclap or something. I always was the morbid one.' She giggled, glancing at Jess. 'She said nothing. She's never got over the road, you know. She wouldn't talk about it. But I've often thought,' Mary said, taking a little girlish skip as if she were out on the playground with the kindergarten class, 'that somebody should go out and check some night, because why couldn't you have a ghost of a tree?'

'At the new moon?'

Mary looked to see if Jess was laughing at her. 'You should go down . . . I'm sorry. Have I scared you, honey? I didn't mean to.'

Jess had shivered, but there was sweat on her forehead. 'I feel a bit odd. It's nothing.' She felt as if her outlines were blurred, her neck swelling, her legs insubstantial.

Dorothy was outside, spraying the rose bushes she had planted at the side of the house where she had resurrected part of the old flower garden. 'What took you so long?' she asked. 'I've left you the table to lay, and the salad.'

In the kitchen, Sybil was feeding the cats. The bird was in his cage, casting seed wildly down at the crouched black and white and ginger backs.

'What took you so long?' she echoed, as if she and Dorothy had been discussing Jess together.

'Aunt Mary was telling me about when they started the road.'

'I'll never forget the day,' Sybil licked the cat-food spoon absentmindedly and threw it into the sink with a grimace, 'when I looked out of the window and
88

saw those men. Will you ever forget the day, Mary?'

'No, Mother. I will never forget the day.'

Sybil cocked her grey head to listen, as she always did
when she spoke or thought of the road. 'Listen to those
maniacs. One day they'll push each other right on off the
end of Cape Cod into the sea.'

'But if it hadn't been for the road,' Dorothy gave the
impression she had stopped in the back hall to listen before she came in, 'I never would have come here, would I?'

'That's right, Dot.' Sybil gave her an extra wide smile.
'That was my lucky day, wasn't it, girls?'

'It surely was,' and 'Yes, Gramma, it was,' Mary and
Jess said dutifully, and Dorothy was able to run the taps,
having heard her due tribute.

But it was our lucky day too, Jess thought, for she
might have had to live with us, the old lady, and God
knows the beginning of marriage is tricky enough without
that. However much you are in love. Especially if you are
that much in love. You expect too much. You expect it
will be the same among other people as when you're
alone. It's not. We're all right at the flat. It's only when
we come here that we begin to hurt each other.

When she was alone in the dining-room, setting out the
silver in the English pattern that irritated Dorothy, a
curious thing happened to her.

In her head, she heard quite clearly three voices. They
were in the middle of a random argument about a film she
could neither recognise nor remember. She was all wrong
in that part. She was lovely, I never knew she could sing
like that. It was dubbed, stupid. It wasn't. It was the
crummiest film I ever saw.

The voices were all English. She listened to them de-
tachedly, automatically walking round the table, laying down

knives and forks, and realised that they were all her own.

I told you it wouldn't work. You didn't. I did, I said leave it alone. It's ruined. There was nothing wrong with it before.

They were discussing a dress she had ripped apart when she was still at school.

I never liked it anyway. That voice went through her head and sounded on the outside, but Sybil walked through the room without looking at her, as if she had not spoken.

Perhaps I am going mad, Jess thought, but when Montgomery came, he said: 'I think you've got flu, Jess.'

'Don't be so professional.'

But he insisted. 'Go on to bed. I'll come up and take your temperature.'

The voices were gone, but when she was in bed, small dynamos rotated in her head after she laid it on the pillow.

'What time is it?' The room was dark.

'Quite late. I came up, but you were asleep, so we had dinner.' Mont switched on the light. She thought that Laurie would have come too.

'The wind's getting up, and Dorothy heard a storm warning on the radio. He and that sterile young man have gone to check the boat.'

'I hope it sinks,' Jess said bitterly.

'That's the spirit.' He put the thermometer in her mouth, and stood looking down at her in such a way that she closed her eyes.

When she opened them, he was still looking at her, his angular face softened, the low ceiling almost brushing his untidy mouse-coloured hair.

Feverish, miserable, wanting Laurie, Jess thought in a panic: I have got to find a woman for him.

8

'IN CONFIDENCE,' DOROTHY said, 'I think the old gentleman rather fancies me.'

'Tell you what, Syb,' Ted said. 'I think she's taken a
shine to me.'

'I knew a woman once,' Dorothy said, 'married very
late in life. Something funny with her insides. They
thought she'd been through the menopause, but she had
a baby at sixty. How do you explain that, Dr Jones?'

'Charming woman, Laurie, very charming. Your
grandmother is smarter than I thought, finding her.'
Uncle Ted had brushed what was left of his hair carefully
across the freckled top of his head, and had brought down
his old quahogging sneakers to be cleaned.

'Why hurry away?' Dorothy asked him on Monday.
'We can put you up for as long as you like.'

We can put you up—in his own family house! 'What's
she up to?' Laurie asked Sybil. 'Had one of us better tell
her he hasn't a cent!'

'How can you be so unkind? Not everybody is as mer-
cenary as you.'

'Jess didn't have anything. I had to pay her fare over to marry me.'

'I didn't mean her. But you'll be glad of my little nest egg, won't you?'

'Don't talk like that!' He took her by the shoulders and held her stiff and glared at her. 'You've never talked like that.'

'I'm sorry.' He let go of her, and she slumped. 'I'm tired, I guess. I don't know what's gotten into me."

'And don't say gotten,' he grumbled at her. 'Don't revert.'

'Don't bully her, darling,' Jess said. 'It's been a tough weekend.'

'She loves to have the house full.'

They talked back and forth across her as if she were not there, as people had been doing increasingly, with the years.

'But so many of us. And that crowd coming in yesterday. And Mary getting her dizzy fit.'

'You're supposed to be sick yourself. Mont said—'

'I'm all right. Mont isn't God.'

'Children, children.' Sybil tapped the rubber of her cane feebly on the floor. She was indeed tired, and though Dorothy had been a marvel, coping, her very energy had sapped what little Sybil still had.

'We are not children.' His eyes were ice blue. 'We are husband and wife, whether you like it or not.'

'Don't talk to her like that!'

'Shut up,' he said to Jess. 'Who's grandmother is it?'

Nevertheless, when somebody—Mary or Ted—raised the idea of taking Sybil to see her stepsister May, who was ninety, it was Jess who had to drive her there.

Laurie was too busy. There was a big property case coming to court. He could not even spare a Saturday, because he had so much work to take home. It was true. But it was also tritely, music-hall true that you married your husband's family.

'I've half a mind to stay after all and come with you,' Uncle Ted said. 'Haven't seen old May for years. She and I used to hate each other's guts.'

'Why don't you?' Dorothy tried once more, but Ted had taken a scare after the bird called out: 'Good morning, Teddy!' in Dorothy's voice, and one of the old men at his club had died at the weekend, and he did not want to miss the funeral. He enjoyed funerals and the obituary notices of his contemporaries. 'Another one gone, heh, heh!'

'I wish I could,' Mary said. 'I've always had a fondness for Aunt May. I was called after her. But who's to get Uncle Ted back to New York? I couldn't drive Mother, in any case, useless creature that I am.'

'Grandpa paid for twenty driving lessons for her once,' Laurie said, 'and after the eighth, the man called him and said he was refunding the balance of the money, for the sake of his daughter and the rest of humanity. "Where is she now?" asks Grandpa. "I don't know." "Where are you?" "Back at the garage. I jumped out when she slowed for a corner and ran for my life."'

'How do you know?' Mary gave Laurie her owl stare.

'I was listening on the other phone.'

'Yes . . . yes . . .' Sybil began to nod her head vigorously, her teeth a little loose. 'I remember. I remember that. Yes, ha, ha—oh, very good.' She went off into cackles

93

of laughter, and Mary said: 'Silly old me,' and smiled, but not convincingly.

From what Laurie had told her of his grandmother, Jess knew about her understanding, her spirit, what excitement and fun they had enjoyed together when he was growing up. Where were the sweet sage old ladies of fiction? Being eighty seemed to bring out all the mean, childish things. Like gin.

'I'll be glad to take Sybil,' Dorothy had said, but Sybil pulled Jess into the corner of another room and whispered: 'Get me out of it. But don't tell her I said so.'

'She wouldn't mind. She knows no one will drive with her.'

'She might be angry.'

Are you afraid of her? Jess wanted to ask, but the whole affair was making her head ache and her legs buckle. She knew that it would have to be her, but all she wanted now was to get back to the apartment and back to bed and make no plans for anybody.

When she had recovered and was back at the office, she drove down to Camden House early on Saturday, and the three of them set off in the smothering heat to see Aunt May, who was in a nursing home at the other side of the State where her son had heartlessly 'put her away', said Sybil, although the son had an invalid wife and five children of his own, one of them a spastic.

Sybil was rather feeble today. She sat at the back, because she said she wanted to doze, but it might have been because Dorothy wanted to sit at the front and watch Jess's speedometer.

She had told Sybil to put on her newest dress and her churchgoing hat, but Sybil had come downstairs, too late to go back and change, in a time-honoured cotton,

94

starched and respectable, like a nice clean old customer in the geriatrics' ward.

Dorothy was very elegant. She wore her blistering pink suit with a straining white blouse which made her look more than ever as if she had stuffed a pillow in her front. Her small feet were puffed over smaller high-heeled shoes, giving her a teetering, topheavy appearance. She had see-thru nylon gloves and a nasturtium hat.

She looked her best in the garden, her lurid lipstick forgotten, in an old smock and flat shoes.

It was a three hour journey. Jess drove in silence, spinning idly through the thread of her memories, and pondering the turns of fate that had joined her to a man for ever, in a strange land, driving two nutty old ladies along the Massachusetts Turnpike to see another who would be even nuttier.

She thought about her 'past', which was short but precious. The few years after school, whose fumbling encounters and tortured disappointments grew more romantic in the memory, more bitter-sweet. If she had not met Laurie, she might have drifted into Steve, who would stay in the Town Clerk's office for years, until he ended up as Town Clerk, and Jess would have had a house like her parents and soon a figure like her mother, and a car full of kids with shiny red cheeks and whining accents they picked up at school, as she had.

Goodbye to all that. She had started life again, burst through the amnion of mediocrity. The British pretended that background didn't matter any more, but it did, oh God, it still did. Here, where no one honestly cared who your parents were, she was accepted for whatever she made of herself, admired for being English.

Your delightful British accent, people said. But she

felt herself talking more like Laurie. Thinking more like him. They sometimes started to say the same thing at the same time, and marvelled, for that did not happen to people until they had been married for years.

She thought about Laurie, and seeing him for the first time with that forehead too broad for the rest of his face, and the bright unused blue of his eyes, talking too much and too fast, gesticulating, making a lot of spit, as he still did when he got going, sucking it back on a pause for breath. Luxuriously, she went yet once more through the saga of their London days, unreeling it inch by inch, like a film savoured over and over again. But before she got to the first very interesting scene, Dorothy had finished her newspaper, and that was it for thoughts.

'Excuse me for being such poor company,' she said, folding the paper into a square and casting it out of the window, for she did not believe in the fifty-dollar fine any more than she believed in the rules of the road. She stubbed out another cigarette into the stinking ashtray, and while Sybil snored gently in the back, regaled Jess with horror stories of the slave labour camp at the department store which she had favoured with her services for so many years. Why had she stayed so long if it really was that bad?

'No one would ask that who lived through the depression. When you've known what it's like to be out of a job —once is enough, thanks very much.'

They pulled off the highway for lunch, and woke Sybil, mumbling on her teeth, and Dorothy drew out the metal liner of the ashtray, and emptied the heap of cigarette ends outside the door of the car parked next to them.

After lunch, Sybil seemed brighter, though still vague. There were days when she should have been left alone to be an old lady with nothing expected of her, but Dorothy would not allow her to age before her eyes, as Sybil did sometimes, when she wasn't trying.

She gave her a grilling about her stepsister, sharpening up her memory and nudging and jollying her along so successfully that Sybil began to remember things she thought she had forgotten, and even, by the time they left the Turnpike at the town where May was 'put away', to look forward to the visit with some gusto.

'May was the pretty one. Always so bright and pretty. And clothes! They were her religion, Marma used to say. I remember a dress she had. She was going to a picnic, that was it. They were all crazy about bird watching then, and they'd go off on nature walks with this gentleman who could do bird calls. Pink, it was, with a big lace collar like a place mat, and her waist nothing. Her beau was waiting in the hall, looking up the stairs for her, and she ran down, just as light and beautiful, and I saw him kiss her, and then she saw me and said: "What are you gawping at, kid?" but she didn't bawl me out like she usually did.'

'Why not?' Dorothy prompted, to keep her alert.

'Because of the boy. She wanted to be cute. She could act anything she wanted to be. Oh, she was a barrel of fun, May was. I could tell you some tales.'

'Do tell.' Dorothy was caking her nose and cheeks with ivory solid powder, through which the veins would soon show mauve.

'Oh . . . I forget. She'll tell you. It will be good to see her again.'

At the nursing home, there had been some misunderstanding about the time. May was being given a bath and would not be ready to receive for half an hour.

Jess went for a walk down the uninteresting road of

shabby white clapboard houses with signs which said Optometrist and Podiatrist and Guests. The owner of the nursing home had a fine rose garden and Dorothy went with her to look at the roses, squatting over the labels and repeating the names knowledgeably, as if she had them all at home.

Sybil went to sleep in the car. When they woke her, she was vague again. 'Go in where?'

'To see Aunt May, Gramma.'

'Oh yes—dear May.'

On the ground floor of the nursing home, rooms opened off a square central hall, where a cocoon of old lady with bandage bows in her hair, and an old man smoking furiously, too close to his moustache, sat before a television screen shot with glaring zigzags.

Dorothy went to adjust the knobs.

'They don't like you to touch it,' growled the old man, and Dorothy drew back her hand and said: 'Pardon me.'

As they went across the hall, slowly because of Sybil, figures watched them hopelessly from the open rooms. A tiny old lady like a chimpanzee in a gay girlish wrapper stood just in the doorway as if she had been forbidden to come out, putting a slippered toe tentatively on the No Man's Land of the hall tiles. Sybil smiled at her and nodded, and Dorothy said: 'And how are *you* today?' like the First Lady at Veteran's Hospital.

Upstairs, in a room which had two beds in it and a smell of faeces, Aunt May lay frail in bed, with rails up, although the outline of her body under the tidy covers looked too insubstantial to move, even as far as the edge.

'Here's your sister!' said the nurse loudly.

Dorothy pulled Sybil forward, holding her arm, and Jess hung back, smiling awkwardly at the second woman

98

who was sitting beside the other bed, but getting no response, and then trying not to look, as she became aware that she was sitting on a commode.

'I asked you, Elsie,' the nurse said cheerfully, and drew the curtain clattering across the rail that divided the room.

Aunt May lay flat as paper, and smiled up at Sybil with her gums, and Sybil leaned on her cane by the bed, breathing heavily, and looked down at her.

'Well, who's this?' asked the nurse, who was big and kind and slate-coloured. 'It's your sister, see?'

'Of course it's my sister,' Aunt May said, with a tiny spark of mettle, like a cigarette lighter in need of a new flint. 'It's my sister Sybil. You look wonderful, Syb. I'm glad to see you.'

She lifted her skeleton's hand, the sleeve of the nightgown falling away from a wrist you could circle with a finger and thumb, and Sybil put out her hand to take it, the two palms touching like dry leaves.

Still holding her hand, Sybil continued to stand and look down at the woman in the bed without speaking, and May seemed content to lie and look, nodding her head to words that did not need to be said. Even Dorothy was a little nonplussed. Things were not lively enough for her, so she said: 'Well!' and pulled up a chair and sat Sybil in it, and then introduced herself confidently to Aunt May, as if the name Dorothy Grue were a household word. She pushed Jess to the other side of the bed and shouted. 'This is the cute little Britisher that's married to Laurie. You remember Loll, of course. Oh, sure you do, that's the girl. Boy, no flies on you, that's for sure!'

She must have been hell as a nurse.

She made some more rallying conversation, and Jess

99

contributed a little. The old lady in the bed, who was not deaf after all, smiled and nodded and said: Yes, yes, and That's nice, and God bless you, and was such easy company that it was a few minutes before they realised that Sybil had not yet said a word.

'Well, come now!' said Dorothy, still master of ceremonies, especially since the big nurse had gone to the other side of the curtain at a tremulous summons. 'What do you say to your sister, eh?'

'My sister?' Sybil looked up at her, her furry eyebrows drawn in with effort. From the other side of the bed, Jess could see her brain trying to work, like arms straining to lift a rock.

'Hullo, Syb,' May said helpfully, as if she were the visitor and Sybil the patient, and Sybil said, very formal, very polite: 'It's very nice to meet you.'

'Gramma—for heaven's sake!' Jess looked blankly across the bed at Dorothy, needing her, unexpectedly, in this predicament.

'It's your sister!' Dorothy bent and hissed into Sybil's ear.

But Sybil, still with the puzzled frown, leaned forward, still very courteous, and asked: 'And where is your home?' the only social conversation she could think of.

'Why—Springfield.' May was bearing up better than Dorothy and Jess, as if she understood better. 'But Plymouth originally, you know that.'

'Oh, that's right. I knew I'd seen you some place before.' Sybil said chattily, and lost interest, looking round the room at the plants, and the family photographs, without recognition, and the towels and plastic bibs hanging behind the door, labelled May and Elsie on adhesive tape. Stricken, clasping her arms as she felt herself beginning to tremble, Jess stared across the bed in horror. Sybil belonged to her life. Her feeling for her was part pity, part protectiveness, part dependence on the stability of her —always there, always welcoming. Now, with the stability disintegrating before her eyes, she realised that part of it was love.

Gramma, come back. I can't bear it if you don't come back.

It was the most terrible experience of my life, Jess heard herself gasping to Laurie. She would hurtle back to Cambridge like a maniac, gallop up the stairs and pound on the door and he would open it at once, because he had been waiting for her, and she would fall into his arms and gasp: 'It was the most terrible experience of my life!' and he would stroke her hair and be proud of her for going through it for him.

The coloured nurse came round the curtain, her white dress stretched tight across her muscular beam, and said: 'How's it going, girls? Having fun?'

'She doesn't know her,' Dorothy mouthed.

'Well, too bad, too bad. That's the way it goes. Perhaps next time you come. We have our ups and downs, don't we, May?'

'I mean the *other one*.' Dorothy turned aside and spoke behind her hand, two nurses together, keeping their sanity by sniggering at the nut cases.

'I wonder if you ever met my father in Plymouth?' Sybil asked, still making an effort to be social, although she was clearly bored.

'Gramma—please!' Jess blurted out in anguish, although she knew she should have kept quiet and seen this through maturely. 'You *must* remember. It's your sister, Gramma dear. Your sister May. You talked about her all the way here. You knew you were coming to see Aunt May. Please, Gramma.'

Please come back. I can't just stand here and watch you go out of your mind.

'She does know you,' she said to the woman on the bed, who was smiling still, quite calm, her paper hands laid like mouse's paws on the fold of the sheet.

'I know,' she said, very reasonably. 'It's all right. I know. Jess. You're Laurie's wife. They've told me about you. I'm very glad you came.'

She held up her hand for Jess to take, and then held up the other for Sybil, as if they were going to swing her up and away off the bed. Sybil got up, and held out her hand without stretching her elbow, and shook her sister's hand with the vague, gracious smile she gave to people in Plymouth she thought she knew, but had no idea who they were. Then she dropped May's hand and looked round for Dorothy.

'Want to go already?' Dorothy said. 'Well, perhaps it's just as well.'

Aunt May squeezed Jess's hand and then let go of it and nodded at her once or twice, her curved eyes hooding over.

'Goodbye, Mrs—er. It was a great pleasure to meet you.' Dorothy unhooked the cane from the back of the chair, and as she propelled Sybil towards the door, Jess heard her whisper coarsely to the nurse: 'Looks like you've got the wrong one in here.'

Burning, unable to look at Sybil to see whether she had heard, Jess glanced back at the old woman on the bed and saw that tears were sliding from under her veined lids and over the ridge of her cheekbones.

MIRACULOUSLY, WHEN THEY got back to Camden House, Laurie was there. He had come down on the bus. Why? He did not say: I couldn't stand the apartment without you. He laughed and said: 'Aren't you glad to see me?'

He was in the back room, with the sunset blazing behind his head and a card table drawn over his knees, strewn with books and papers.

She saw him at once, through the open doors of the kitchen and the hall and the dining-room, and while Sybil and Dorothy were fussing at each other on the way in, Jess ran and flung herself at him: 'It was the most terrible experience of my life!'

'Watch out.' He clutched at his papers while she hugged him frantically, until he fended her off and looked at her. 'What's the matter?' But as she began to tell him, he looked over her shoulder and said: 'Hello, Gramma. How was the trip?'

'Wonderful. I'm never scared with Jess.' Sybil paused in her shuffling trot into the room to see if this had registered with Dorothy, but Dorothy was in the kitchen, turning knobs on the stove in a masterful way.

'I'd forgotten you were coming, Laurie,' she said happily. 'Fancy me forgetting that.'

Jess opened her mouth to say: He wasn't, but Laurie grinned and said: 'You forget all the important things.'

'Don't I though?' Sybil dropped into a chair and leaned her head back with a gusty sigh. 'Pour me a glass of sherry, there's a good boy. I'm quite exhausted.'

She was exhausted! Who had slept for nearly two hours in the car, going and coming, and only woken long enough to go crazy.

'Don't forget to offer one to Dorothy,' Sybil said, as she always did, for although Dorothy and the sherry bottle were old friends, she pointedly waited for an introduction when anyone else was there.

'What happened?' Laurie asked Jess, at the cupboard in the corner. 'What's the matter with you?'

'Come outside. Please come outside. I've got to tell you.'

'The car?'

She laughed, right in his face as he turned with the bottle. Neither of them cared a straw about the car, except as a boring necessity. When she tore the chrome strip off one side, she forgot to tell him for weeks, and when he found it, curling in the trunk, he threw it away.

'Come outside.'

He looked at her through the heavy-rimmed glasses he wore when he was being a lawyer, which Mont swore had plain glass lenses. 'I'm working.'

'You were.' She pulled him through the room and out of the side door. Outside, she leaned against the cypress tree at the corner of the house, breathing with her mouth open, staring at him.

'She didn't know her. That's what happened. She talked about her all the way in the car, and then when we got there, she didn't know her.'

'What did you expect? The poor old bat must be over ninety.'

'Not May. She knew. But your grandmother. She didn't know her own sister. I'm glad to meet you, she said, and she asked her if she'd ever met her own father.'

Flat. The nightmare that had boiled in her all the way home, waiting to spill over in release, fell flat. He shrugged and said: 'So what? She never should have gone all that way.'

'You asked me to take her!'

Who was going crazy? All the way home, she had fermented, saving the story for him as they saved all the incidents of their day to spill out, interrupting, gabbling, in the excitement of coming home to each other at night.

'I thought you'd want to hear.'

'I do.' He put his hands in the pockets of his cotton trousers, although she was aching for him to put them round her, on her. 'I do, honey,' he said, with a patience that was worse than anger, since he never called her honey except when he was imitating the kind of married couple they did not want to be. 'But not if you're going to make fun of her.'

'I'm not making fun of her. It was Dorothy who—'

'Dorothy what?'

The worst thing she had been fermenting for him all the way along the endless, soul-destroying Turnpike was what Dorothy had said to the nurse.

You've got the wrong one in here.

And in the car . . .

'In the car,' she began, and pushed herself away from the tree to stand against him.

Sybil had kept silent for a long time, while Dorothy chatted inconsequentially, and rushed the radio full volume from station to station, too fast to get anything but howls and bellowed syllables and claps of song. At last, she leaned forward and asked Jess: 'Who was that poor woman who claimed she was my sister?'

'She *was*. She was your sister May.'

'Don't play games with me. I know my own sister, I should hope. I'll show you a picture of May when we get home, then you'll know.'

It would be the picture on the stairs, May laughing and

shaped like a figure eight, in her wedding dress with a train like a carpet and her hair cushioned out.

'Yes, Gramma.'

Dorothy said nothing, but made catarrhal noises in her nose and clicked her teeth a little. They fitted better than Sybil's, but when they both clicked them at meals, it was like dining in the boneyard.

When Jess heard Sybil snore, she glanced over her shoulder to make sure she was asleep, and said to Dorothy: 'I'm very worried.'

She sounded middle-aged to herself, saying that, fusspot. She had a vision of her mother, pressing a hot water bottle at the sink to make the air spit out. 'I'm very worried about your father,' if he sneezed twice.

'I think she ought to see Montgomery, don't you? She's never been like this.'

'She doesn't need Doctor Jones.' Dorothy never called him anything but Doctor, even on Sundays. 'She has me to take care of her.'

'Yes, but—' Jess stopped being middle-aged and fussy. She was young and inadequate and . . .

And frightened, she wanted to tell Laurie. I thought she was *glad*. She was glad about what happened to Gramma.

That was the most terrible part of the whole terrible day. But now, suddenly, she could not tell him. It would be petty, mischief making, hysteria. He would think she was trying to make trouble, common, suspicious, like her mother and her friend down the street when they talked with hisses and side glances.

'In the car what?' He put his arms round her.

Dorothy opened the kitchen window and went: 'Yoo-hoo!'

He swore. He could not stand her, but passively. She was here. She was necessary. He could put up with her. He would never understand the flame of hatred that had leaped in Jess as they were going out of the room in the nursing home, with May weeping silently and the big nurse snickering. And had leaped again in the car when Dorothy said: 'She has me,' and smiled.

She could not tell him. He kissed her, but she was chill and passive with disappointment.

'Well, O.K.' He dropped his arms. 'Let's go back in.'

'How was Aunt May?' he asked Sybil casually.

'I don't know.'

'Why? Did she die before you got there?'

'Don't say things like that. May's not dead. She's as fit as I am.'

He made a face at Jess that said: You see, and went back to his card table.

'Did you see her today?' Jess asked Sybil, loudly, to make him listen.

'See who?'

'Aunt May.'

'What about her?'

Jess took a deep breath. 'You saw her today.'

'Well, you say so.' That was Sybil's way of agreeing and disagreeing at the same time. 'I slept so much in the car, I daresay I forgot.'

'But, Gramma.' Jess knelt before her and took her dry hands. 'You remember when we were in that room at the nursing home. And in the bed there was a woman who—'

'Leave her alone, Jess,' Laurie said. 'Don't bully her.' He ran a hand through his black hair, rested his head on the hand with the fingers spread, and started to read again, remote, unconcerned.

107

'All right.'

Jess went upstairs to their bedroom. Were they staying the night, or what? He had not brought a bag. But they kept a few things here, an old razor, toothbrushes, sweaters, since they came so often. Jess felt heavy and defeated. It was too great an effort to go downstairs and ask him: Do you want to stay the night?

If he was reading, he would not look up. Or perhaps he would look up and through her. She could not reach him. She could not communicate. What had happened? She stood in front of the high bureau that served as a dressing table, and stared and stared at her face in the oval mirror in the dark wood frame on the wall.

Why should he love her? She examined every inch of her face, analysing the structure of the eye, the nose, the way the pale mouth moved when it opened, smiled, closed over the teeth. She stroked her cheeks, pulled back the corners of her eyes, pushed her light hair back from her rounded, childish forehead, then hit it back down again, pulling it into points impatiently between thumb and finger.

How do I look to him? She tried to see herself from outside, and thought she looked like just another girl, immature, uninteresting. Why should he love you? she asked the unexciting, unexotic face. I wouldn't, if I was a man. She stared woodenly for a few moments longer, and then, in a kind of flat despair, turned away and went out of the room into the hall over the stair-well.

I never noticed there was a mirror there.

She saw herself, head and neck, a few yards in front of her, very clearly, the round brown eyes surprised, the mouth unsure. The fair hair was untidy, pulled raggedly down in points. Not bad though, not bad at all. Not pretty, an interesting face, exciting, sexual. If I was a man . . .

She opened her mouth. The mouth of the image opened. She turned her head and saw the other head begin to turn, but when she looked back, it was gone. There was no mirror on the wall.

I saw myself.

9

In September, the great trees round the house seemed to deepen, heavy and rich with green, in the pause before they kindled, and the fire crept imperceptibly through them until they ringed the house with a blaze of colour that made motorists exclaim: Why go to Vermont? whether they meant to go or not.

Day by day, the yellow house looked paler among the fantastic scarlet and orange and gold. It was the season when Papa said: 'We must have the house painted this year.' But when the leaves faded to ochre and fell, and the house stood revealed on the dying grass for the first time since the start of summer, the yellow paint looked brighter, and brighter still when the snow came, and so he would let it go. 'Till next year,' he would tell Marma, 'when there are not so many expenses outside.' But she would rather see money spent on the house than on the grounds and nurseries, and there were always expenses outside.

One year, he dammed the stream which ran from a spring under the hill through the corner of the pasture to the pond, and made an ornamental pool, with seats and spouting frogs and water lilies. Sybil worked with him when Ted was away at school. She took a pair of Ted's corduroys and put them on behind a bush out of sight of the house, and took them off before she went in, and Marma would say: 'You can't have worked very hard, you didn't get your skirts muddy,' although she would have been angry if she had.

'In looking on the happy autumn fields,' Sybil remarked to Dorothy, panting a little as they went through the gate and up the slope, 'and thinking of the days that are no more.'

'You can say that again.' Dorothy trudged beside her in a pair of stiff blue jeans she had taken to wearing in the garden, rolled several times at the bottom, for anything that would accommodate what she called her waist was much too long in the leg. 'Though I wouldn't have my time again, if it was handed me. It was different for you, of course.'

Sybil agreed, although she privately thought that she had worked far harder than Dorothy in bringing up three difficult children and a grandson, and helping Theo with the land here all those years.

She was taking Dorothy to see the place where the ornamental pool had been. The stream had long since broken the dam, and destroyed all the stonework over the years, carrying most of it away down the slope to be buried in undergrowth. Now there were only a few lumps of broken masonry, and part of one of the stone frogs, embedded in the tufty grass.

Dorothy was not very interested in the few Roman remains. She was afraid Sybil would start to reminisce about her father, which always aggravated her, so she pottered on farther upstream, and Sybil sat down heavily on a stone and waited for her, trying to look at her beloved house without looking at the cars flashing behind it forty-three to the dozen, as if the idiots did not know that Labour Day was long come and gone.

'Eureka!' Dorothy came sturdily back down the hill, the same shape as the frog in those pants, holding in one fist a plant with a thick hairy stem and big dark lily leaves. 'Hellebore. Why didn't you tell me it grew here?'

'I didn't know you wanted it.'

'You did so. What do you think I've been dusting the roses with all summer? You won't catch Dorothy Grue buying those expensive chemicals when Nature has given all her resources into her hand.' (She got that bit out of Will Camden's herbal notes.) 'Itchweed, they call it. Here I've been making do with those few roots I found by the old rain tank, and had to go so easy with it the Japanese beetles sat up and laughed at me. Listen here—with this little lot by the stream, time I get them dried out, we'll have enough rose dust to last us for life. Your life anyway.' Dorothy planned to live a whole span after Sybil. In this house? Sybil sometimes wondered.

But she was a worker, you must give her that. This summer and fall, she had spent so much time outdoors that Sybil had often been lonely, sitting idle under the trees in the long chair, or alone in the house with Roger and the watching cats, who were not nearly such relaxed pets since they had the bird on their minds.

Some companion, Sybil would think to herself, some housekeeper, as she poked about the kitchen, looking into the ice-box and the oven to try to guess what Dorothy was planning for lunch. Some companion. And yet when the weather was bad and Dorothy was in the house all day, talking, knitting, bossing, putting dustcloths into Sybil's hand, or settling her on the ugly plastic stool with the ironing board at sitting height, 'to keep you from getting rusty', Sybil would wish she could get her out of the house.

There you were. There was no pleasing some people, she thought, meaning herself. 'That's what happens to you when you get old,' she told the bird, slyly rattling the bars of its cage with a spoon, which Dorothy forbade her to do on account of Roger's nerves. 'You don't know what you want.'

Like a baby. But if you had to become a baby, why couldn't life be arranged the other way around? If you started as an old woman, people would put up with you as a novelty, knowing you would improve. Then you could end up as a fragrant baby, and everyone would dote on you and never think you were a nuisance, however much attention you demanded.

Sometimes when she was too much alone, she would think about telling Laurie or Jess that Dorothy neglected her. But when she saw them, she forgot. Or if she remembered, it did not seem to matter anyway, once there were people around. It only mattered when she was alone for so many hours that her thoughts curdled; but then there was no one to tell.

Just as well. Since they had taken her to that sad place where the old man did not dare touch the television and the little monkey lady did not dare step out of her room, Sybil had got to be extra careful.

If Dorothy quit, she herself might end up in a place like that, caged in a bed like that poor woman upstairs, with a stranger using the commode right under her nose.

Why had they taken her? Not Jess's fault. Sybil was sure of her now. She was on her side, and Sybil was ashamed to remember that she had once imagined her an enemy. She could remember that. One did not forget the contemptible things.

It had been Dorothy's idea, obviously. Something that was said—in that bedroom? in the car?—gave it away. They had taken her there to try to trap her into saying that poor woman was May—May, with her bounce and style!—to prove she was senile. Then they could put her away like that, in a place where people went out of their minds, because it was expected of them.

But she wouldn't be caught like that, oh no. Didn't know her own sister! But she must be very, very careful. Hold your tongue, Musket; so she did. Laurie would not understand anyway. He did not understand things like he used to, in the old days when he was her boy. She had always fought for her own company. He would think she was jealous now of Dorothy's strength and energy. Which she was. But the woman had a right to her own time, and you couldn't help admiring her for what she achieved. All talk and no do, shan't be said of Dorothy Grue, was one of her dictums.

She had done wonders with the flower garden and the rose bed, and her herbal project was going ahead splendidly. Apart from the rose dust, which she made, following Papa's notes, from the dried root of the plant called false hellebore, she had prepared a medicine for her cough, using the old bilberry and wild parsnip mixture which Sybil and her father had tried on the cows, and she intended to exorcise with the juice of milkweed the honeycomb wart which had recurred on her thumb for years, like the bloodstain in a room of murder.

She also had a cure for the ache in Sybil's leg, which she made by boiling chopped horseradish, mixing it with barley and oil and applying it as a plaster. Very soothing, when she did not put it on too hot. The time she did, she was quite pleased, since it gave her the chance to try out her burn treatment of stewed ivy leaves.

She was currently working on a project to get rid of the liver spots on the backs of Sybil's hands with the juice of wild carrot tops mixed with powdered pumice. 'Will remove any marks on the skin whatsoever,' John Camden had written. It had done nothing so far but give Sybil a slight itch she never had before, with which Dorothy would deal as soon as she had gathered enough sorrel.

She had made a good harvest this autumn, laying out her leaves and pods and roots to dry in the old seedhouse. Some of them, like the milkweed and the hellebore, which were poisonous, she crushed and pounded up there, but she brought most of them down to the house, which pleased Sybil, for she had not felt like climbing the hill for months. Be honest, Syb. You haven't felt capable of going up there for over a year. Since you broke your fool leg.

She enjoyed the herbal project, and did not mind being experimented on in the cause of science. It kept Dorothy happy, and when Dot was in a good mood, life was fair. When she was in a bad mood—well, there it is, we all have our off days.

And when it was an on day, she could be so great, joking, easy-going, spoiling Sybil with extra comforts and little surprise presents. When Laurie and Jess made faces about Dorothy, or laughed at her, Sybil found herself defending her abruptly, although in solitude, with Dorothy pottering on the hill and forgetting lunch, she had imagined the three of them cosily discussing her.

Once when Dorothy had a weekend mood—unexpectedly, for she was usually amiable when the children

115

were there—Laurie asked Sybil with a serious face: 'Are you really happy?'

That would have been her chance to say . . . what? There was nothing to say.

And she did not say much about the remedies. Laurie and Jess were sceptical, and Montgomery disapproved ('Natch,' said Dorothy), so at weekends they stored away the equipment, and used aspirin and mercurochrome, as if they had never heard of such a thing as being Pilgrim herbalists.

But when the young ones were not there, 'We work like clam diggers,' Dorothy told Maud Owens. 'Sybilla has burned the bottom out of three pans, making syrups.'

'You really mess about with that stuff? What's in this jelly?' Maud put down her hot biscuit.

'Don't be silly, Maud. Melia made that batch.' Sybil usually loved visits from old friends like Maud, with snatches of recaptured anecdotes and allusions that did not need explaining. But today, she found herself almost wishing that Maud would go, so she could start crushing bilberries.

Dorothy allowed her to do all the simpler operations, like crushing and bruising, and pressing out on the little corrugated board strips of paste to be rolled into pills. She would sit in contented peace at the kitchen table, pounding the pestle in the mortar, while Dorothy stirred, glassy-eyed at the stove, with the bird perched on a warming shelf above, whispering and chattering like a witch.

Dorothy always made her decoctions and syrups on Priscilla, although it was a trouble to light, and the kerosene made her wheeze. But if they were to be Pilgrim maids, they could not make herbal remedies on a gleaming white electric stove with enough buttons on it to run a battleship, although some of them were fakes. On each side of the black central stovepipe, graceful wrought iron trivets could be swung in and out to warm dishes over any of the hot plates. Here Roger perched, exchanging banalities with Dorothy, and picking up his feet nervously, like soldiers marking time, if the stove below was too hot.

One evening when Dorothy was going to brew the borage syrup which had replaced her morning prune juice, she stood on the stool and opened the door of his cage, but he would not come out, even when she put her thick finger invitingly at the entrance, like a waiting taxi.

He was huddled at the far end of a perch, his plumage ruffled and dull, his flat bright eye lidded like a syphilitic.

Dorothy put in her hand and pulled him out, which he hated. He liked to go everywhere under his own steam. When he obeyed one of Dorothy's chirruped orders, it was because he wanted to do it anyway, not because 'he knows everything I say'.

Holding him tightly, for he would fly back to the cage if she let him go, since it was not his idea to come out, Dorothy brought him under the light. His eyes were gummy, the lids swollen.

'Oho. That's how it is. Poor fellow's been in a draught again. He wishes some people would close the door when they make all those trips out to the trash can.' But it was her ashtrays that Sybil was constantly taking outside, since Dorothy never emptied them until they were brimming. 'Hold him a minute, Sybil, while I go and consult the good book.'

Sybil did not like holding the bird's smooth, curiously muscular body, any more than she liked the feel of him clutching her finger with his feet that had a reptilian texture, but a surprising animal heat.

117

While she was holding him, he struggled, and she let him go, afraid of breaking a wing. He fluttered clumsily because of his eyes, dropped down instead of soaring up, and in a streak of black, the big panther cat had half his tail.

There had been some bad moments in Sybil's life, but this was one of the worst. When Dorothy came into the room, Roger was back in his cage, scolding like a blue jay. The feathers were on the floor. The cat crouched, yellow-eyed. Sybil's hand was empty. No good making excuses. She had been given the bird to hold. She had let him go. Trembling? You crazy old fool. She can't kill you. What are you afraid of?

And Dorothy, a casket of surprises, did not say a word. Her globular glance took in the whole story. Her crimson mouth tightened, the lipstick running off in little tributaries in the creases of the skin around her lips.

'I'm sorry, Dot.' Hellfire on being eighty, when you couldn't control your voice! 'It will—it will grow again quite quickly, won't it?'

'Bay leaves,' Dorothy said, in her normal, grue cigarette voice. 'For a cold in the eye, make a lotion of bay leaves.' She had a bunch hanging over the stove. She picked off a few, and got to work without another word.

Dorothy did not speak much for the rest of the evening. Despising herself, Sybil found herself making bright, sycophantic conversation. Who was it? Mary. Poor Mary, when she was a child, used to do that with her to try to find out if she was still angry.

Dorothy was non-committal, neither angry nor mollified, picking her teeth thoughtfully behind her hand. When the bay leaf lotion was cool, she applied it deftly to the affronted bird, then unhooked his cage from the ceiling and carried it upstairs to her room, his special treat, hitherto reserved for his birthday, and for the Fourth of July, to show Jess that even a bird could celebrate release from the British.

Nobody said: Bedtime, Sybil. She waited for a while to see if Dorothy was going to make her hot drink, but although she could hear her moving about upstairs, she did not come down. Feeling about a hundred, Sybil found her cane, which seemed to have a life of its own these days, and started up the stairs.

No wonder her mother was waiting for her at the top of the stairs in the plumed hat and the busty paisley button-through. Bella Camden had never missed an opportunity to make a bad situation worse. In the brief moment, when she knew for certain that her mind had gone, Sybil heard Dorothy's chuckle and cough, without registering it.

'Just a bit of a joke.' Dorothy stood in the doorway of Emerson's room with her hands folded in the sleeves of her harsh scarlet robe like an Oriental. 'Just a bit of a joke to liven things up.'

THE BAY LEAVES did not work on Roger. Two days later, he was still rheumy, and sneezing on a note disconcertingly like Dorothy's. She told Sybil: 'Your father evidently didn't know much about birds.'

'He did. He knew all their calls. I remember one winter

—you should have seen the snow we had those days—
something very rare came to the bird table for the suet.
A yellow something or other. He wrote to the Audubon
Society.'

'What did they say?' Dorothy often missed the point
of a story, carrying it on beyond its denouement to anticlimax.

'They said good, I suppose, I don't know. Who are
you calling?'

'Dr Jones. It says in my budgie book that infection of
the eye can be cleared with penicillin lotion.'

'Why not the vet?'

'All vets are butchers.'

When Sybil had a sore throat and Montgomery had
given her penicillin tablets, Dorothy had washed them
away down the sink and given her rose hip linctus.

But the bird, that was different. The bird must have
penicillin.

When Montgomery arrived that evening, tired and in
a hurry, for he was fitting the visit in quickly during a
slow labour at the hospital, he was surprised to find Sybil
sitting at her desk writing a letter.

'She said she was very worried. What's she playing
at?'

'Didn't she tell you who it was for?' Sybil began to
laugh. She took off her glasses and mopped her eyes with
her sleeve. It was really excruciatingly funny, especially
Montgomery's face when Dorothy came bustling in like
a hospital nurse specialling a V.I.P. and asked—no, told
him to prescribe penicillin for the bird.

'You're out of your mind,' he told her brusquely.
Imagine daring to talk to Dorothy like that! 'I'm up to
my neck in babies and tonsils and a flu epidemic, and you

call me out here for that moulting carrion. Take him to the vet.'

'Dorothy doesn't like vets,' Sybil said, pulling her mouth into seriousness.

'Dorothy can go—'

'Hush, Montgomery.' Dorothy had marched out of the room, but she would still be listening. 'Come on now, it's good to see you, anyway. You haven't been near me for two weeks, you know that?'

'You haven't invited me.'

'You never used to wait to be asked.'

'She doesn't like me.' He made a face and jerked a thumb over his shoulder.

'Of course she does. She likes everybody,' Sybil lied. 'It's my house anyway,' she added, compounding the lie, but she drew courage from Montgomery with his untidy cow-lick hair and his long restless limbs. 'Get yourself a drink, dear.'

'I can't stop. I've got a woman—'

'Just a minute or two.' Sybil did not want him to go. Dorothy would be upset about the penicillin.

He telephoned the hospital to see if he could stay a short while, then poured himself a large whisky and fell into a chair with his legs stuck out and his shoulders almost on the seat, and closed his eyes.

'Poor fellow.' Sybil came and sat by him. 'You work too hard.'

'I've been up a few nights. It's nothing.'

'Not at your age. In ten years' time, you won't be able to drive yourself like this. I'll have to find a good woman to take care of you, after I'm gone.'

'Aren't you going to be here in ten years?'

'Not the way I'm going.'

It was strange. When she was a long way away from being as old as this, she had thought it impossible to contemplate her own death, much less talk about it. Now, she did not mind. In fact, Montgomery said, she talked about it too much.

'It gets very boring,' he said, 'when people keep on about dying years before they actually do it.'

'I know.' She had learned that to say: When I'm gone, or: I shan't be here much longer, gained you no sympathy.

'You're a smart woman, Sybil Prince,' he said. 'I wish my grandmother had been like you.'

'What was she like?'

'I've told you.'

'Tell me again.' She liked to hear about Montgomery's wretched grandmother, who used to insist on coming to his mother's parties, and then sat around in the living-room with tears rolling down her face, telling everyone how miserable she was. She liked the comparison with herself, for Montgomery's whistle on the driveway was always for her, and he would come ambling through the house calling: 'Where's Sybil?'

When he had to go, Sybil went with him to the kitchen and gave him a spoonful of parsley to chew, so that the woman in labour should not be gassed by his breath. He said goodbye cheerily to Dorothy and told her to try boric acid, and he kissed Sybil, and she stood at the back door to wave him away in his little roaring car.

'You know what I think about that young man,' Dorothy said, in statement, not question.

'You mustn't mind about the penicillin, Dot.' Sybil had her pacifying voice on again. 'Perhaps it's unethical for him to treat birds.'

'Nix on that,' said Dorothy, harking back to Junior

High. 'I was going to try boric acid anyway, so there, Mr Know-it-all. But that wasn't what I was going to say.'

'What then?' She forced you to lead her on, even if you would rather let it drop.

'I think he's after your money.'

Sybil laughed. 'That's really funny, Dot. That's really a laugh. I haven't got much, anyway.'

'But would you leave it to him?' Dorothy asked intently. Did she have designs on it herself?

'It's for Laurie. Everything. Not that there's much of anything. But Montgomery—good heavens, Dot. Fancy you thinking—'

'You pay a lot of attention to him,' Dorothy said sharply.

'Of course. I love him.'

'Mm-hm.' Dorothy nodded, lips closed, racehorse nostrils flaring.

'What do you mean, mm-hm?'

'You love him like you love Laurie, huh?'

'Is there something wrong in that? I hardly ever see my other grandchildren, and they haven't much time for me when I do. Montgomery is a bit too old, I suppose, but I wish he *was* my grandson.'

'Doesn't look like it.'

'Why not? You know how fond I am of him. He doesn't come here as much as he did, because—' she looked at Dorothy. 'Because he's so busy.'

'Maybe that's just as well,' Dorothy said darkly. 'Maybe that is just as well, because I sure do hate to see old folk making fools of themselves. I sure do hate to see that.'

When Laurie came, his grandmother wanted desperately to tell him what Dorothy had said, but she was too ashamed. Suppose there were some truth in it? A fool of herself. She was austere with Montgomery on Sunday, and would not play checkers with him, as they usually did.

'Even if I let you win?'

'I don't care to, thank you.'

It had been so much fun to flirt with Montgomery a little bit, chiding him, letting him tease her, swerving, for his benefit, from imperious dowager to lovable child. All this time, when his casual, humorous young presence had added so much to this old life of hers which he had fought to give her back, had she been merely making a fool of herself?

'What's poor Mont done?' Jess asked.

'Nothing, I hope, except tend to his business. Is it a crime suddenly, if I don't want to play checkers?'

She worked on her sewing all afternoon, while they were outside cutting up a fallen tree for her winter firewood. She was mending a sheet, putting in a patch with the small meticulous stitches she could still manage if she pushed her glasses down her nose. Outside the window, she could hear the chock, chock of the axes, and their talk and laughter.

Jess came staggering in with a laundry basket full of chips for the wood-box by the fireplace. She moved with the load pregnantly, stomach out, but Sybil had given up fretting about that. They knew their own business.

Jess put down the basket, and pushed back her forelock with a hand powdered a rich brown from rotting wood. 'It's lovely out,' she said, and Sybil nodded to the critics who nagged within her: There, you see, I didn't hurt his feelings. I did him a good turn by not keeping him indoors.

When they were gone that night, she and Dorothy saw all their favourite Sunday programmes, and had a nip of bourbon in hot water with sugar, as they sometimes did if they stayed up late and felt cosy.

Dorothy was at her nicest. 'Happy day?' she asked at bedtime.

'Very happy. And you?'

'I'm always happy here with you,' Dorothy said. 'You know that.'

10

THE BAD WEATHER came early that year. It had been possible in some years, Laurie said, to sit outside in the midday sun at Christmas. But already, by November, great lashing storms of wind and rain had driven in from the sea to strip the trees of their last colours, and litter the lawn round the yellow house with broken branches.

By early December, it was already very cold, and the sages of Plymouth, which meant anyone who had been there five years and had a gift shop or a bar with driftwood and fishing nets on the ceiling, prophesied a Long Hard One.

The weather was the reason why Laurie and Jess did not come down so often. There was not the same point in escaping from town if you had to stay shut up in the house with Dorothy's catarrh and the bird's imitation sneezes and the old trees groaning like a ship, and scrabbling at the roof.

Once one of the tall sycamores blew down across the driveway, and they had to leave their car there and go back to Cambridge on the bus.

'Why do they never blow the other way?' Sybil complained. 'Why couldn't it have blown down across the road and wrecked a few cars?'

'Because the wind comes from the sea,' Dorothy explained equably. She could never be persuaded to join in vituperation against the scourge. Brought up in a city, she could not see the tragedy. The cars going by through the night past the front bedroom were company, she said, when she could not sleep. (What about Emerson?) She liked to think of all those lucky people going to quaint Cape Cod. Although she never went across the Canal herself, since to her the Cape spelled her brother-in-law, and that was bad news.

So when Sybil called and asked when they were coming, or when Laurie said to Jess or Jess said to Laurie: 'We must go to see Gramma,' the weather was a safe excuse for putting it off. Not only an excuse to Sybil, but to each other. There were certain things, even at this stage of their closeness, that were not spoken, and Jess did not know whether Laurie had faced the curious fact that at Camden House, his real home, it was easier to hurt each other.

When this realisation first intruded on Jess, it seemed absurd. But looking back, it became more true the more she thought about it. Did he know? She wanted to ask him, but she could not. Why is it, she wanted to say, that our life together in this cramped, shabby apartment is so perfect, but at Gramma's house, which is old and beautiful and stuffed with years of happiness, we spoil it?

They hardly ever fought at the flat, and if they did, it was half comic, never vicious. But at Camden House, beloved, familiar, Laurie's boyhood skin, they seemed to have at least one small piercing fight every time they were there.

On their last weekend, it had rained all Saturday. Sybil was in bed with a cold, being given tansy tea by Dorothy, and Laurie and Jess had fallen into a stupid argument about the British herb and the American erb. They never argued about pronunciation. It was one of their triumphs over other Anglo-American couples they knew. So why now? Jess put on the mule face which Laurie said reminded him of her father, and later became frigid and averse.

'You should have married an American girl,' she said, when he complained.

Only Dorothy was happy that weekend, whistling off key all the old Broadway numbers of her youth long gone, and rubbing peanut oil into Roger's growing tail feathers in the most sickening manner.

That Sunday, Jess heard again those curious voices in her head, three of them, and all her own.

She had risen early, leaving Laurie asleep, and was walking round the house drawing back curtains. Dorothy was a great one for secrecy at sundown, and was haunted by the fear that a passing motorist might see her in her slip and come storming in off the highway to rape her.

Window by window, Jess let in a cold grey light that promised snow, and looked without enthusiasm at the day.

When Laurie woke, would he have forgotten yesterday, or would he remember how stubborn and sulky she had been? If she went upstairs now and knelt by the bed and woke him to say: I'm sorry, would he say that he was sorry too for haranguing her like a prosecuting counsel, enough to make Dorothy carol to Roger: 'Birds in their little nests agree'? Or would he accept her apology, assuming grandly that it was her fault?

Why should he always be right?

He was cleverer than she was, better educated, better read, he had spent his life among people whose ideas did not all come from tabloid dailies and whose conversation was not limited to food and racing and a piecemeal dissection of the neighbours. He would be a brilliant trial lawyer one day, the Senior Partner had told Jess, and Laurie was not even impressed, because he knew it.

If I'm not good enough for you, she thought sickly, why didn't you find that out in London, since you're so clever?

You're being unfair, he said in her head, or she said it, and it was then that the voices began.

I told her what I thought about it, and she agreed. She always does. She's got no mind of her own. I don't know how she keeps the job. Job. Fob. Lob. She keeps the job. She won't much longer.

Whoever they were discussing, it was not her and Laurie.

All three voices were her own, not the way she sounded when she held the flaps of her ear down to see how she sounded to other people, but the way she sounded to herself when she was speaking. But she was not speaking. She was not even thinking. She was listening quite dispassionately to the three English voices, light, desultory, rather boring.

In the last column you put the figures for the net cost of each item. I put mine in the first column. That's the part in red. He said separate net from gross by one column

129

of figures. That's what I did. You diddle. I did. Take Robin now, he's a good example. I knew his mother. She lived in that house where the bus stops.

Running fast, as if she could outrun the voices, Jess tore through the rooms and up the stairs.

'I'm sorry—oh darling, I'm sorry!' She flung herself on the bed.

'You're trembling,' he said, holding her, and she kept her face in the pillow so that he could not see that she was crying.

During the week, Sybil called them. 'Dorothy wants to know if you're coming on Friday. Her sister might come.'

'What difference? Has she got a disease?'

'Ssh.' The grandmother giggled. Dorothy was probably in the same room. 'It isn't that, but—you know.'

Oh yes, they knew. It was a question of presuming. Dorothy's sister would not presume, etc. So if they said they were going, she would have a grievance and not go near the place for two years, and would eventually come to believe that she had been refused entry, even though she had refused it to herself.

Or would it be Dorothy who took offence, and walked out? Disaster. Her grue was worse than her bite, and Gramma actually seemed to like her, which showed how your faculties could degenerate.

Jess put her hand over the mouthpiece and asked Laurie: 'You don't want to go?'

He shook his head, so Jess told Sybil that it might snow again, which should satisfy everybody, and probably discourage Dorothy's sister.

'Ought we to?' Laurie's conscience about his grandmother came in flashes, usually too late.

'She didn't mind. She'll have Dorothy's sister. Better value in that. And it really might snow.'

'Yes, it might snow.'

'But . . . there's something else, isn't there?'

'Don't say it,' he said quickly. So he knew.

'Yes, I must.'

'Don't. If you don't talk about fighting,' he said childishly, 'it makes it not matter.'

How could he think that? they were worlds apart still. So she lied perversely: 'I wasn't going to talk about it. I don't want to.'

'What is it then?'

'It's—' She would tell him about the voices. She had thought she would never tell him, or anyone else. She thought if she never spoke of them they would not come again. Why—she looked at him, astonished. That was just his reasoning, about the fighting. We are closer than I thought.

'Tell me.'

'I can't. You'll think I'm going mad.'

'If you are, I may as well know it.'

'The first time, I thought it was the flu, but then it happened again when I wasn't ill.'

She told him about the three voices which were all her own, and he listened seriously, and chewed on his lips and drew down his dark brows, and said omnisciently, like a psychiatrist: 'You're tired, that's all it is. I've got to get you out of that office. They're driving you.'

She shook her head. The work in the Admissions office at the college was leisurely and pleasant. But he repeated: 'It's because you're tired. It doesn't mean a thing, I'm sure. No more than a ringing in your ears. Don't let it scare you.'

131

'It doesn't, much. That's what is so odd. I listen to them quite calmly, as if it was an ordinary, rather boring conversation that everyone else could hear. It's only when I realise I'm doing that, I panic, and then they go. Do you think I ought to see—see somebody?'

'God no.' There must never be anything wrong with her. He could have chills and headaches and sprained fingers. She must be as strong as a horse. The time she had flu, he thought Mont was exaggerating when he told him what her temperature was.

'I think you're imagining things, my dear,' he said rather patronisingly, so Jess retorted: 'All right then, listen to this. I wasn't going to tell you, but one night at the house—one night—it was the day we'd been to see Aunt May and you wouldn't believe me about what happened. You were downstairs. I went up to our room, and stayed there looking at myself in the mirror for a long time and wishing I was someone else.'

'Who?' he asked, with interest.

'When I went out of the room, I saw—I saw a ghost of myself.'

Laurie laughed, and she laughed too, in relief. She had meant him to be impressed, but now it was more reassuring that he was not.

'Only Sybil sees ghosts.'

'I did.'

'Emerson?'

'I told you. Myself.'

'Maybe it was my great-grandmother. She deserved to be a displaced soul. You can't see a ghost of yourself, darling.'

'I saw it.' She described the momentary vision. How it had looked like her, and moved, and seemed in some

132

way to be under her control. 'Like a reflection, only there isn't a mirror there.'

'That's it. You said you'd been looking in a mirror. You looked for so long that the image was printed on your eye. Yes, that's it.' He began to talk fast, gesticulating. 'Listen, here's how it is. If you look at a light bulb, you can still see it when you look away. Dark, like a negative, but you see it. Try it. You can do it with anything, if you stare hard enough. I'm looking at that doorknob.' He fixed a ferocious blue stare on the brass doorknob, counted twenty, and then switched his head quickly round. 'There—there it is. Over on the wall. It's white. See it?'

'Of course not.'

'Nor could anyone have seen your ghost, unless they'd been staring at you too. Dorothy.' He giggled. 'Suppose you looked like Dorothy and came face to face with yourself. That would really rock you.'

His explanation was so logical and satisfying that Jess was not afraid any more. She had not been afraid at the time, strangely, any more than she had been afraid of the voices. It was only afterwards that her skin began to creep.

Thanks to Laurie, she thought no more about the apparition. Until about ten days later, when for no reason it came into her head in a shop, and she stopped dead in the crowded ground floor aisle and stared at a display of hectically coloured bags that no one in their senses would carry.

The light bulb was reproduced black. The darker doorknob came out white.

The head and neck of herself which had hung before her over the stairs had been colourless, like a dream, but the hair was light, the eyes and mouth dark. It was not a negative.

'Can I help you?'

'How much are the bags?' she asked, and moved on without hearing the answer.

'BUT YOU'VE *never* missed my birthday!'

'Gramma, I've told you. If it were any evening but the twelfth. If I don't go to this dinner, I'll get shot. I don't want to—a bunch of politicians sounding off at each other in Neopolitan dialect. But Guthrie said, "You'll go with us," and he means it.'

'You'll be glad to know,' Sybil said unfairly, 'that I'm bitterly disappointed. It may be my last birthday.'

'She'll probably live at least ten more years,' Laurie told Jess, 'but she makes me feel like hell. What shall I do?'

'I'll go,' Jess said, although she did not want to. 'It won't matter if I'm not at the dinner, but you must be.'

'Birthday dinner with Sybil and Dorothy. You might roast Roger.' He groaned. 'I can't let you always do my jobs for me.'

'It's all right. Don't worry, darling. I like to do things for you. I would kill myself for you, if it would help.'

He looked at her quickly, and saw it might be true. 'I never had a wife like you,' he said. 'I'll skip the dinner.'

'No, you must go. I'll be all right. I'll come right back after they go to bed.'

'I don't like you driving so late.'

'I'm not helpless.' But sometimes he liked to pretend that she was. So she agreed to stay the night and drive back early in the morning.

'Ask Mont,' Laurie had said. 'Be more fun for you.' But Mont was at the hospital, and could not come to the telephone.

Jess arrived with a car full of presents. She had something for Dorothy, and a new toy for Roger's cage, which was almost as important as remembering the nylons and earrings for Dorothy.

'Where are all the cats?' She realised that six o'clock had come and gone, without the familiar sight of Sybil pottering back and forth between the can opener on the wall and the dishes on the counter, ankle deep in mewling, undulating bodies.

Sybil looked at Dorothy. 'They live in the barn now,' Dorothy said. 'They were too much trouble for Sybil to take care of. And always under her feet. We were afraid she'd trip over them and break her other leg. I knew a woman who fell over a stray cat on the steps of the public library, and split her skull from neck to crown.'

'It wasn't because of Roger's tail?' Jess asked Sybil, not Dorothy, but Sybil's face was blank, and Dorothy answered: 'Don't be so petty, dear.'

'How do you keep them out?' Sybil's cats were as much a part of the house as the pictures on the walls or the smell of old woodwork.

'Just don't let 'em in.'

Dorothy was pouring drinks, and they were toasting Sybil, but Jess could not blot out the vision of anguished whiskered faces outside the windows, claws scrabbling at the glass, and Dorothy pulling the curtains across on the outer darkness where there should be weeping and gnashing of teeth.

Maud Owens came to dinner, and an elderly couple whom Sybil had known all her life. Dorothy had roasted a turkey and made a cake like a temple, and Sybil had been with her to the liquor store and chosen the champagne herself, since Dorothy's tastes in alcohol ran to communion-type wine and California port.

Maud was amusing and the elderly couple were charming, and it was much gayer than Jess had expected. After Maud had driven the others recklessly off up the driveway in a blast of blue smoke, she said: 'It was a lovely party.'

'Except for one thing.' Dorothy's mouth closed as if she had drawn a string round it.

'What?'

Dorothy shook her head without unfastening her mouth. 'Bedtime Sybil,' Roger whispered raucously, as she took the china mug from the dresser, rattling it purposely, and Sybil said: 'One of these days I'll go to bed when I please and not when that bird says so.'

Dorothy went up with her, and when she came down, Jess asked her: 'What do you mean—except for one thing?'

Dorothy sank the wattles of her chin into her watermelon bosom which had encroached so far on her waist that it was arbitrary where she put a belt, and raised her eyes to fix them on Jess.

'You should know, dear.'

'You mean because Laurie couldn't come?'

'The first time he's ever missed, she said.'

'It isn't. Two years ago, he was in England.'

'The poor old lady.' You could not argue with Dorothy,

because she merely bulldozed on, as if you had not spoken. 'She took it very hard.'

'She took it very well. She had a wonderful time tonight. I haven't seen her so bright and gay for weeks.'

'Ah—tonight,' Dorothy said. 'The juice of the grape hath miraculous powers, hath it not? I wish my herbals would work as quickly.'

'But he couldn't come. She understands that. I know she was disappointed at first, but she'd never try to get in the way of his career. After all, she paid most of his way through Harvard.'

'Did she indeed?' said Dorothy. 'That's very interesting. I wonder why she never told me.'

Jess did not say: Because it's none of your business, or: It might give you ideas about her money, although both thoughts occurred to her. She said: 'But that's not why he's good to her,' which was a thought that might have occurred to Dorothy. 'He loves her, you know that. I love her too. That's why I came, and I think it almost made up to her for Laurie.'

Showing some bice green slip and a lot of fat veined leg, Dorothy climbed up on the stool and opened Roger's cage. He flew onto her shoulder, balancing with a lift of his wing as she climbed awkwardly down, and muttering into her nest of black hair, which she wore pulled up all round into a puffy roll.

'Listen—why should you worry about it, Jess?' she said. 'No man is worth making yourself miserable over. I learned that years ago when I lost mine.'

'I'm not miserable.' Sometimes Dorothy made far less sense than Sybil.

'I wouldn't blame you if you were. Eighteen months married, and your mother three thousand miles away. Jess

137

will go down to Grandma like a good little girl. Very convenient.'

'If you mean—' Jess's body filled with heat. She could feel it burning up into her face.

'I don't mean anything.' Dorothy mumbled her lips in and out, and the bird pecked bluntly at them, a parody of kissing. 'What are you trying to put into my mouth, you naughty girl? Is that all the thanks poor Loll gets for being so thoughtful and insisting you stay overnight?'

Jess went out. She ran upstairs and into her room, and sat down on the bed, breathing hard. She was very angry. But when she started to think about it, Dorothy had not really said anything. It was she—she herself who had interpreted the silly little digs into full scale scandal.

But it was true he had jumped at her offer to come. And he had insisted on her staying the night. They had not been apart for a night since their marriage. Why now? Her mind churned like dirty wash-water. She hated herself. But the germ of the idea was there. She had let it in. She fought, but it was disgusting that she should even have to fight. If he ever knew, he would kill her.

Or I would kill myself. She got up wearily from the bed and turned to pull down the cover. She felt very tired, drained of strength, the movements of her muscles unreal and meaningless. Before her, on the other side of the bed, she saw the head and shoulders of Jess, her face screwed up and pale with misery, her eyes staring at nothing.

Poor girl. The image made an attempt to smile, as she made her mouth move towards a smile. She was wearing the white blouse, fading out towards the waist. Jess thought of it as She, a separate thing, and yet there was again a sense of possession, almost of power.

She stared at her. The other She stared back. They

138

could stand there staring until the end of the world, eyes trapped in eyes, but with no thought behind them, for thoughts took up moments of time and this was suspended in a timeless space with no relation to past or future.

Touch me. Jess lifted her right hand and reached out. Across the bed, the image reached its left hand forward. Her hand became cold, numb, as if all the life had run from it. The hands met, but there was no feeling. Jess closed her eyes to stop the image staring, and when she opened them, there was nothing there.

It was not until Jess realised that she was standing in a familiar lighted room, staring blankly across the bed at nothing, that the terror invaded her like an icy hand, her own chill hand, feeling its way through all the courses of her nerves into the last secret chambers of her brain.

She heard Sybil's stick, and through the doorway she saw the old lady, in the quilted rosebud dressing gown that had been one of her birthday presents, navigating slowly back from the bathroom to her room.

'Gramma!' Jess went to her.

'What's the matter, child? You're panting.'

'Am I?' She stopped, for the panting was not involuntary. 'I ran up the stairs.'

'When do the young stop running and start walking? How do you like me in my grand new robe?' She struck a little attitude of vanity, making the face with which she tried on things before the mirror, and it was all so familiar and safe and dear that Jess kissed her, and hugged her hard, because the chill and the terror had vanished, as if nothing had happened.

But it had happened. And this time she had not been looking in a mirror. She had seen it, and she had not been afraid of it. Not at the time. That was why the fear came afterwards—because she should have been afraid.

'Do you believe in ghosts?' she asked, when she was tucking Sybil into bed.

'I'd better.'

'You told me you'd heard Emerson breathing in there.' She jerked her head towards the room that was now Dorothy's.

'Hush,' Sybil said. 'They told me not to talk about that. I can't remember why, but I remember they told me.'

'Because they thought you frightened me.'

'Was that it? Oh well.' Sybil had got her teeth out. She looked smaller in bed, as old people do, as if the mattress sapped her. Her jaws caved in and the sockets of her faded eyes were red with fatigue. Over her brindle hair she wore the familiar turban made of a linen dish-towel depicting the Trooping of the Colour that Jess had sent her from London before they ever met. What can one send Americans that they haven't already got? And then she had seen the dish-cloth, in dozens of designs, in Boston department stores.

'They thought I imagined the breathing, you see.'

'Oh well.' Sybil's attention wavered. She reached for the jar of dubious smelling ointment which Dorothy had prepared for the skin on her hands.

Jess asked quickly, to get her back: 'Have you ever seen a ghost—here, in this house?'

Sybil nodded. She was rubbing the cream in circles, nodding every time the fingers came round.

'The house is haunted then?'

'Now then, now then, what's going on here?' Dorothy charged in, just like Miss Driscoll charging into Five B although she used to know what was going on because of the spyhole in the door.

'Is the house haunted?' Jess repeated, for she had to know.

What did Sybil see? What if it—oh God, what if it was a spectre of me, appearing for years, perhaps even before I was born?

Sybil would have cried out at the first meeting: 'But I know you!'

Jess thought back, and saw Sybil that first day, coming towards her with a smile of welcome. Or of recognition. 'She's just what I thought she'd be.' That's what Sybil had said, as if she had seen her before. 'She's just what I thought she'd be.'

The old lady did not answer. She lay on her back gumming the insides of her jaws and watching Dorothy, who was folding clothes which Sybil had already folded.

'A haunted house, don't be ridiculous,' Dorothy grumbled, shaking out a corset with a rattle and a snap. 'I've no time for such nonsense myself, and I wish you wouldn't put ideas in Sybil's head. I've trouble enough with her as it is.'

'Am I a trouble to you, Dot?'

'Well, it's not all roses around here sometimes, I'll tell you that,' Dorothy said, in case anyone should think she had it made.

Jess was not going to sleep in her room, not until Laurie was there in the bed with her. She would not see anything if he was there. She did not know how she knew that, but she felt sure of it.

She would rumple the bed and sleep on the sofa downstairs and get up before Dorothy came down. First she was going to write a letter. She was going to write to Mary and ask her for the truth.

Mary used to have nightmares in this house. Mary

knew all the old legends. Mary had seen the Charity tree weeping under the new moon.

What else that she had not told?

Dear Aunt Mary,
I am terribly troubled and disturbed, and only you can help me.

She wrote a long letter, telling Mary everything. She told her everything that she could not tell to anyone else, for they would think she was losing her mind. Mary would understand. She would not pass it off as imagination, or being tired, or gazing in a mirror. The night before the wedding, when Jess had screamed because there was someone lying beside her on the bed, Mary had been the only one who did not tell her it was a dream. She had stood shyly at the back of the crowding, well-intentioned fuss, wearing a raincoat over her night-dress and looked calmly through her owl spectacles at a scene which was no more than she expected.

The letter was almost finished when Jess heard a car crunch on the gravel at the back of the house. The knocker fell cautiously.

'Jess—Laurie? Anyone up?'

'Oh—Mont.' She ran to open the door, which Dorothy had bolted and chained like a fortress for the night. 'Oh, I am glad you came!'

'I brought a present for Sybil. I knew it was her birthday, because last year Melia made that marvellous cake, remember?' He was holding a box foolishly wrapped with bows and tendrils of ribbon. 'I'm sorry it's so late. I saw your light from the road as I was going home, and then I saw your car. Where's Laurie?'

'He couldn't come. He had to go to a dinner with Mr

142

Guthrie, so I came to be at Sybil's party. I wanted you to come, but I couldn't get hold of you.'

'I was at the hospital all last night and most of this morning, I think. I've lost touch of time.' He passed a hand over his face, and as they went into the lighted sitting-room, Jess saw how tired he was. His eyes were shadowed, and his face was grey, and pricked with beard.

'Sit down.' She pushed him into a chair and picked up the unfinished letter to Mary and crammed it into the pocket of her skirt before she knelt to make up the fire.

'Babies?'

'A kid.'

Jess turned her head. His lower lip was pushed out over the top one. His hair, which was never properly cut, stuck up at the back. His eyes were leaden and sad. 'What happened?'

'He broke his arm a week ago. Nasty mess it was, but I thought he was doing all right. He came through the operation well, and the fever wasn't unusual. I didn't worry about it too much.'

He leaned forward, dangling his bony hands between his knees and talking into the fire. 'Last night, I got scared. The antibiotics didn't seem to be touching him. I took him to Children's Hospital in Boston this morning. I've been there all day. They're still not sure what the bug is. It could be a—well, God, Jess, they were talking about gas gangrene.'

Jess sat back on her heels and looked up at him. 'Whose fault?' In England, if something went wrong, most people accepted it as more or less an act of God. Over here, she had learned, it must always be someone's fault.

'Not the hospital,' Mont said quickly. 'Mine. He was

playing near a stable. It was a compound fracture—very dirty. I should have spotted it.'

'But he'll be all right.' She tried not to make it a question.

'The father came with me to Boston. After the people up there had seen the kid, the father asked one of them whether there was any chance of not being able to save the arm. He said: "Look, Mr Dennis, it's no longer a question of saving your boy's arm. It's a question of saving his life." I wish I hadn't heard that. I knew it was true, but I wish I hadn't heard that.'

'I'll get you a drink.'

'Yes, please. Would you make it rather big?'

She poured him enough whisky to knock a horse out, and then sat on the floor again by the fire. He said: 'This is good,' and sighed, and closed his eyes. After a while he reached out and pulled her shoulder, and she sat leaning against his chair while he stroked her hair, absently, but with pleasure, as if she were a favourite dog.

'Why aren't you in bed, Jess?'

'I'm not going to—I wasn't tired.'

'What about the Dolly sisters?' he asked. 'What would they say?'

'They're fast asleep. And there's nothing to say anything about.'

'That's the hell of it.'

Jess turned and looked up at him.

'You know what I feel.' He turned her round again so that she was not looking at him, and kept his hand on her neck. 'Everyone keeps on at me about Mont's got to have a woman. Montgomery must get married. We must find a good wife to take care of Dr Jones. I used to think so myself. But you spoiled it.'

'Please don't.'

'I wish I didn't like that guy you married. It's an immortal situation. What a cliché. The best friend hanging onto the dregs of hope.'

'We'll never break up, if that's what you mean,' Jess said rather breathlessly.

'It gets tough though, huh? Marriage, I mean. After the first excitement.'

'Yes,' she said cautiously.

'Happy?'

'Not terribly. Not at the moment.' She blinked. It would be ridiculous to cry, because she was getting a little sympathy. And treacherous, since the sympathy was not impartial. 'I hated myself tonight.'

'I hate myself every night,' Mont said lazily, 'and most of the morning too. What was the matter?'

'It was Dorothy. She started hinting things about Laurie. At least, I thought she was hinting.'

'Bitch. She won't speak to me since I refused to give her bird an enema. No loss, but I don't see Sybil enough. Did you push her face in?'

'I wish I had. But I listened, and I even thought about what she said, and enlarged on it. That was what was so horrible. The thing is—I don't know, is there something about this house? We seem to fight when we're here. Over nothing. Is it the house? Or is it that being with old ladies gets on our nerves? If so, that's hateful. Do you believe there could be something in the atmosphere of a house that affects people?'

'Not this one. People are happy here. Remember last Christmas, how marvellous it was? I never had a Christmas like that.'

'Nor me. I used to look forward to the time when this

house was ours and we would live here when Sybil—' Her mother's rubric that you brought ill luck to a person by anticipating their death died hard—'eventually. Now I'm not so sure.'

'The only comfort I can offer you,' Mont said, 'is that with me, you'd be worse off. I'll probably never have a decent house, let alone a haunted one.'

Jess got up. 'Do you think this house is haunted?' she asked, making it casual.

'By Dorothy Grue.' He said her name like a shudder, and closed his eyes.

'You ought to be in bed. Poor Mont. It's awful for you about the boy.'

She thought of the child, sweating with fever in the Boston hospital, imagining an arm already putrefied and blackening. And she had dithered introspectively when his anxiety was so much greater.

'Go on home and get some sleep, if you've got to be in Boston early,' she said, but he was asleep in the chair.

11

SYBIL WOKE IN the small hours of the morning, as she often did, and lay for a while telling herself a few of the old stories.

For some years now, she had been talking to herself out loud. Not because she was a raving lunatic, but because she liked the sound of her own voice.

It was not senility. It had nothing to do with the mumbling old men who shuffled along sidewalks wagging their heads at an invisible audience. If I want to talk to myself, I'll talk to myself, she told her audience, who were always pulling her up and calling her silly old fool and useless old person. For reminiscence, it was far more satisfying than mere thinking. Thoughts got confused, but if you put words out on the air, they stayed in place.

The stories she told to herself were not the same as the ones she told to Dorothy, which were mostly plain anecdotal recollections, with no moral or motive. To herself, it was a saga of self-justification, an apologia in which Sybil Camden Prince was always right.

It wasn't my fault . . . I didn't break my leg on purpose,

after all. Crippled up . . . but there was nothing wrong with me until I fell. I always took care of myself. Ask anyone. Sybil can take care of herself, they said; it's a marvel what she gets through. She invented the thirty-hour day. Well—I raised three children and took good care of Theo and nursed him all through the end. No one nursed Theo but me. I could do anything those days. Didn't I milk the cows right through the war after Benny was drafted? Didn't I milk for Papa? He said: She's a better milker than any man on the place, Papa said. I've done anything. All my life I've put my hand to anything, and if it wasn't for this leg . . . nobody knows what I've been through with it. They don't know, and I'm glad for them. I wouldn't want my worst enemy to suffer as I've suffered.

She stopped talking and thought for a moment. She had no worst enemy. She had no enemies at all. She didn't have an enemy in the world.

And that's a lot more than you can say for most people, she told the ceiling, for the pillow had slipped down under her neck and her head had fallen back, but she could not be bothered to raise it.

Nights like this when she lay awake, watching the tree outside her window come imperceptibly into detail as the night faded, she always used to go into Emerson's room and put a hex on the cars.

It was a waste for Dorothy to be in there. She did not mind the cars enough to lose any sleep casting spells at them. Well, there was always the bathroom. With groans and gasps and cries of: 'Oh—oh', which were purely trimming, for she was not in any pain, Sybil sat up and swung her legs carefully over the side of the bed, rubbing her scarred thigh perfunctorily, like a mechanic wiping a greasy hand on his overalls.

Below her, she heard the back door open. She heard Jess say something, and then to her surprise, she heard Montgomery's voice. Was someone ill! Jess? Dorothy? It was three in the morning by her luminous clock. It couldn't be three in the afternoon, because it was dark outside, she reasoned shrewdly.

'Be sure and call me tomorrow,' Jess said. Montgomery answered something that Sybil could not hear. The car door slammed, the starter rattled a couple of times, and then he roared the engine, called out again to Jess and drove away.

This interesting interlude had made Sybil forget why she was sitting on the edge of the bed with her legs dangling over her slippers like a fireman ready to jump into his boots. Montgomery was gone, so there was no need for her to go downstairs, if it was her he had come to see. She swung her legs back again, pulled up the covers and curled up to sleep in the evocation of that far ago womb.

'WELL! WHAT SHALL we two girls do today?'

Sybil was tired, with a vague recollection of having been awake for rather a long time in the night. But Dorothy was full of pep and energy, and the old house shrank from her assault with mop and duster, like a fragile patient at the approach of the Pride of the Nursing School.

Anna Romiza still came on Tuesdays and Fridays to

clean, but this did not quell Dorothy. On Mondays and Thursdays she had to racket round so that Anna should not label her a messy housekeeper, and on Wednesdays and Saturdays she had to racket around doing all the things that Anna had neglected. On Tuesdays and Fridays when Anna was there, Dorothy was pretentiously integrated, which was trying for Sybil, who had never thought about Anna as coloured before Dorothy drove it home.

'I hadn't thought about doing anything yet,' answered Sybil, who was still thinking about whether her breakfast was going to digest, or stay for ever in her stomach like pebbles in a bag.

She stared, put a hand to her mouth and belched discreetly, saying: 'Pardon me,' as Dorothy had taught her, although she had believed all her life that it was not wrong unless you called attention to it.

'Those old gas pains again?' asked Dorothy delightedly. 'You know what we've got for *that*.'

She had the leaves of the willow tree that hung into the pond, bruised with pepper and steeped in wine. She had the decoction all ready prepared in a Coca-Cola bottle labelled Sybil: Gas.

'I don't want it.' Sybil made a face. 'It tastes bad.'

'Natch. No medicine that was tasty ever did anyone any good.' Dorothy put the glass of tainted wine in front of Sybil. 'Drink it, dear.'

'I don't want to.' Swimming out of memory, came a picture of herself sulking over milk, her mother standing over her in a fury.

'Come on, drink up!' Dorothy said brightly, and Roger swung on a blind cord and chattered: 'Drink up, Roger kiss Mother, Sybil Sybil Sybil.' He liked the sibilance of her name. It mixed in well with the chirps and twitters that peppered his talk when he was in two minds whether he was a bird or a person.

'It will make me feel worse.'

'Drink it, I said.' When Dorothy spoke like that, her eyes bulged as if they would pop right out of her head on-to the floor. Her mouth was a scarlet bar.

Sybil drank, belched again, and clapped her hand across her face, as the wine came back sour and nauseating into her mouth.

'You bring that up, I'll give you some more,' said Dorothy lightly. 'I'm going away off up the hill now to get some parsnip root so we can make up some more of my cough pills.'

If she gave up cigarettes, she would not have the cough, but Dorothy Grue would smoke in her coffin, she threat-ened, and now that she had discovered the herbal joys, she cherished the cough as an excuse for pill-rolling.

'Watch those beets while I'm gone. It's your saucepan, you know, if you let them burn the bottom out.'

Sybil did not know whether to be glad or sorry that the willow and wine mixture had worked. It would have been nice to be able to tell Dorothy on her return from the seed-house: I told you it wouldn't do me any good; but on the whole it was nicer to be rid of the indigestion.

Dorothy did not return anyway, not for quite a long time, and Sybil began to feel panic. Had she walked out? There were times, she admitted to herself, oh yes, there were times when she would not have been sorry to see her vanish into thin air, go up in a puff of her own tobacco smoke. No other way for her to go without someone's feelings getting hurt.

But only to think of her not being there brought a

frightening emptiness. What would happen to my life? I cannot do without her, Sybil thought, trapped and sick with anxiety, like a woman with a brutal lover.

If she had walked out . . . she often threatened it. 'One of these days, I'm going to walk right out of this house and see how you get along without me.' Sybil always laughed, but with the uneasy feeling that it was not really a joke.

She had been angry about the medicine. She had walked out. What shall I do, left here all on my own with no one to know or care? I can telephone for help. But then if she comes back and it turns out she's only been for a walk, what kind of a fool shall I look?

Just in time, she remembered the beets, and trotted, limping with the effort of haste, into the kitchen to snatch off the pan with a wildly beating heart. Saved by the bell! But Dorothy was right. It was her pan. If she wanted to burn it, she'd burn it. Burn the bottom out of every darn pan in the place and she couldn't say boo.

It was easy to be bold about Dorothy when she was not there. When she was, it was easier to stay in her good favour. Pleased that there was something she could do to help, Sybil drained off what little water was left in the beets, and squeezed them in the old wooden press that she had found in the cellar, getting a considerable amount of beetroot juice on her clothes as she worked.

One of the things Dorothy had gleaned from the note-books of Sybil's father was that if you sniffed beetroot juice up your nose, it would restore a lost sense of smell and also cure bad breath, if you had it.

Dorothy would not agree that she ever had bad breath, but she had lost much of her smelling power from years of chain smoking. So every now and again, she would soak wads of cotton in beet juice and stuff it up her flaring nostrils which were red to start with, but now like a vision of hell.

The Congregational minister had come visiting once when Dorothy was giving herself the smell treatment. She had gone to the door like that, and when he saw her with two magenta pools in the middle of her face he cried out: 'Has there been an accident?' and clutched his heart, for he was almost as old as Sybil, and not as strong.

When the juice was made, there was nothing for Sybil to do but worry, and when Dorothy eventually came back, with a small jar full of whitish powder, she said: 'Where-ever have you been? I've been quite worried.'

'Thought I'd poisoned myself at last? No such luck, Sybilla.' Dorothy was in a much better mood after her trip up the hill. 'The storage jar up there was almost empty. It was warm as a greenhouse with the sun pouring in, so I stayed to pound up a whole lot more of the parsnip root. If we're in for a rough winter, I'm going to need it.' The fiction that her cough was bronchitis was always preserved.

The pills were made by mixing the powdered root with the pulp of boiled bilberries which had been mashed and stored in a jar when the berries were ripe. Dorothy then added a large amount of honey, and enough cornmeal to bind the whole mess together in the scarred old wooden bowl which was part of the cult, like Priscilla.

'Can I roll the pills?' This was a great treat, allowed only to good girls. But Sybil was a good girl now, because she had drunk the sickening wine and it had cured the indigestion.

She sat very happily at the table, rolling the paste into strips along the corrugations in the pill board, and break-ing off neat little lumps which she revolved between finger and thumb until it was 'a perfect pillule!' Dorothy popped one into her mouth and rolled it round with bulging eyes of pleasure, as if it was a candy ball. Sybil knew they did not taste very good, because she was fed one every time she cleared her throat, but Dorothy pretended they were delicious, so that Sybil had no excuse for making a face.

Roger coughed. Was it possible that he was clever enough to connect the cough with the pill? Dorothy believed he was.

'Of course you shall, my pet.' She wedged one of Sybil's pills between the bars of his cage, and he took an indiscreet peck at it, and then fell to cleaning his beak frantically on the perch, as if he were sharpening a carving knife.

'Roger all better!' Dorothy told him. 'We don't need that stupid old Doctor Jones, do we?'

Doctor Jones. Montgomery. Sybil paused with a pill half rolled, still bullet shaped between thumb and finger. What did that remind her of?

'Funny thing, Dot,' she said. 'I just remembered. You weren't sick in the night, were you?'

'Never sick nor sorry, that's Dorothy Grue.'

'How about Jess?'

'She was all right when she went off this morning. What are you getting at? Did you hear something in the night?'

'Montgomery—' Dorothy turned quickly to look at her. 'Oh, nothing.' She moved her fingers again to roll the pill.

'Montgomery what?' But Sybil was not going to say any more. Silly old Gramma she might be, but instinct was instinct and she still had it with the best, and her instinct told her now to keep her mouth shut.

'He sent you a present, remember? Cheap looking thing, I thought, but some might like it.'

'Yes, it was lovely. I've forgotten what it was. What was it?' Dorothy had lost interest and turned away, but Sybil was still flustered.

'A china cat. Fancy forgetting what Doctor Jones gave you, of all people! Though he might have had the courtesy to come in and say Happy Birthday dear Sybil. Leaving it on the doorstep, like a baby. I wonder when he came by.'

'Oh, I know.' It was not often that she knew something that Dorothy did not.

Dorothy turned round again and was staring at her intently, her red mouth slightly open, her convex eyeballs glittering. 'What do you mean? You're hiding something. What are you getting at, lady?'

'I can't tell you.' Not when you look at me like that. I can't tell you.

'Tell me.' Dorothy moved towards her and Sybil clutched the edge of the table, because she was afraid.

She shook her head. 'There's nothing to tell,' she said weakly.

'Tell me, I said.' Sybil could see herself in Dorothy's eyes, two tiny old ladies in pink sweaters transfixed in the shining iris. 'He was here last night,' she said. 'That's all. I heard him talking to Jess.'

'What did they say?'

'I don't know. I heard Jess say: "Be sure and call me tomorrow".'

'What time was this?'

'About three.'

'Why didn't you tell me?'

'Oh—' Sybil shrugged her shoulders, and then slumped

them forward. She was suddenly very tired. 'I forgot, I guess. It's not our business anyway.'

'No.' Dorothy began to move away, still keeping her eyes on Sybil, though the eyes were not looking at her now, but backwards into her own head as she stepped backwards. 'It's like you say—none of our business.'

12

When Jess found out at the end of February that she was pregnant, she was so happy that it seemed that all happiness in her life before had been a mere frivolity.

She felt that all of a sudden she mattered. The world could not do without her. Laurie could not do without her. She had never mattered before. Driving on the Expressway which hurtled cars in and out of Boston three abreast like a chariot race, death if you hit, she had thought sometimes that she could be gone without trace. She would leave no mark at all. Her parents would grieve conventionally and go to church two or three times, but it would not affect the pattern of their existence. The wound in Laurie's life would close over after a while. He would still become a brilliant lawyer. He would marry a second girl and not insult her with memories of the first. It would be as though Jess had never been.

But now—now she was important. She was going to do something—was doing it already with every pulse beat she shared with the foetus—that would make her remembered for ever. As someone's mother and grandmother and great-grandmother, she was a vital link in the saga that ran back through and beyond the *Mayflower*. Posterity could not do without her. Laurie could not do without her.

He was overjoyed. 'You'd think no man had ever been a Daddy before,' Dorothy said, but she said it benignly. Everyone was all of a sudden more benign, more affectionate. Sybil rallied out of the vague, uncertain lassitude that had been creeping over her, and became more sensible and alert, as if she had quickened with the quickening of the baby.

Dorothy, who had been growing more bossy as Sybil grew more senile, stopped bullying her, except in a joking, comradely way, which Sybil quite enjoyed. She liked the attention of Dorothy bustling her about, and checking up on her at all hours of the day. What's she doing now? Lay off that salt shaker—with a heart your age! You wear that undershirt one more day, it will walk right out the door. She liked the freedom from all decision and responsibility which Dorothy's dictatorship ensured.

For a while, Laurie and Jess had been afraid that Dorothy was after Sybil's money, but a few staged conversations to let her know there was not much had made no difference. In their absorbed excitement over the baby, however, they forgot the slight nagging worry that Dorothy was getting power drunk.

And Jess began to forget fear. The voices and the visions did not return. She could remember that she had been afraid, but she had forgotten what the fear felt like, and she was not afraid of its return. Her ghost had been laid. The last time she had experienced the horror of seeing herself was the night before she conceived her child. It had come to life when she and Laurie had come together again at the apartment, rushing hysterically home from work as if they had been parted for a year.

The child had exorcised the ghost. Jess talked no more about the house being haunted, and she thought of it no more. There was nothing to remind her. The atmosphere had changed to greet the splendid changes within her.

Montgomery was just as delighted as everybody else. Jess had always said that she would die rather than be his patient, and he said that was a good thing, since he already had twice as many maternity cases as he could handle.

Then suddenly, it was all gone, the vessel shattered and the happiness run out and seeped away.

It was at the end of a Sunday in March. A soft blue day that was a rehearsal for spring. Laurie and Mont played golf, and Jess walked round with them, picking out the clubs she thought they ought to use, and enjoying the exercise as dutifully as walking the baby after it was born.

Sitting on the bench at a tee, waiting for Mont to find a wildly driven ball, Laurie said: 'I never thought of you as beautiful before.'

'I'm not.'

'You are now. Is it because we are so happy?'

She nodded, holding his hand down with hers on the bench. 'You see me differently.'

'I see you very clear,' he said. 'Oh God, we're lucky.'

When it was time for them to leave the yellow house, she could not find him. She thought he was outside with the car, so she put on her coat and said goodbye to Sybil and Dorothy, who was on whisky tonight, for some reason, and very cock-a-hoop.

She kissed Mont in the kitchen and turned, laughing at something he said, and saw Laurie in the doorway with his hands in his pockets, hunched and glowering.

'Where were you?' she asked, going to him. He put out

a hand and pulled her outside, pushed her roughly into the car and drove off without saying a word, his profile hard and almost unrecognisable.

'What's the matter?' He did not answer. She had seen him angry before, but never like this.

'Where were you?' she asked again. Something had happened. He had met somebody. What had happened to him?

'On the hill.'

'Why?' She put a hand on his arm.

He shook it off. 'Shut up,' he said. 'We'll talk at home.'

In spite of her dismay, Jess went to sleep. Caught in the predicament of his rage, she still could fall asleep, although it would be better to be killed awake, and he was driving like an idiot.

Safely in Cambridge, by some miracle, they went up the stairs of the old brown brick building in silence. Laurie shut the front door behind him and pushed her into the room, where she stood clasping her hands in the middle of their beautiful shaggy orange rug.

'All right,' he said. 'How about it?'

She waited, and let him talk. After a minute, she asked: 'Who told you this?' quietly, because he had been shouting, and it had sapped all other sound.

'Sybil.'

'Oh no—no, she would never do anything like that. I don't believe it.'

'Why not? Why shouldn't she? Don't you think it would hurt her too?'

'She isn't like that. What are you doing? You're making something up.'

'All right then,' he said. 'It was Dorothy.'

Jess sat down. 'Tell me. Tell me what she said. Don't

shout at me. I have to know exactly what she said.'

She put her hand on the sofa beside her, but he sat down on the other side of the room and put his head in his hands. When he started to talk, low and flat, like a child repeating a lesson, he did not look at her.

HE HAD BEEN alone in one of the rooms after supper, trying to finish the Sunday paper before it was time to leave.

Dorothy came in and started to talk, which was a compulsion with her when she saw anyone reading. She croaked on rather disconnectedly about nothing much, and he thought she might be a little tight. She sat with her legs apart and her skirt drawn back over her fat doughy knees, and there was a sort of glitter to her eyes, as if he had discovered how to manufacture pep pills out of her herbs and simples.

'Jess looks well, doesn't she, Loll?' She lit a cigarette and coughed as if her lungs were coming up—'I don't know when I've seen her look so well.'

'Nor I.' He lowered the paper and smiled at her, because she was saying: 'What a lovely girl she is. I'm sure she's going to have the loveliest baby that anyone ever saw.'

She wasn't a bad old sack really. He went back to the editorial, and it was while his face was behind the newspaper that Dorothy said: 'Better be sure it's your baby.'

'What the hell are you talking about?' He threw the

paper down, and she was smiling, the tip of her pale tongue just showing between her teeth, her head on one side, like a bird.

'It's not my business. I wouldn't want to interfere in what isn't my business. It just seems funny to me, that's all.'

'What seems funny to you?'

'All this time married—why wasn't she pregnant before?'

Laurie got up in a cold fury and went out of the room and banged the door on her. The woman was drunk, or mad, and he should not even have listened that far. He went to the doorway of the dining-room, and stared through at the back views of Jess and Montgomery doing dishes together at the sink. Then he went back into the front room, where Dorothy was sitting just as he had left her, knees apart, head on one side, smiling, as if she had known he would come back.

Sick, distraught, hating himself even more than he hated Dorothy, he said: 'Go ahead then. Tell me.'

'IF YOU CAN believe that,' Jess said heavily, 'you can believe anything.' She felt as if she were made of lead, hardly able to speak for the weight that was on her.

'You don't deny that he was there?'

'Of course I don't deny that he was there. I told you about the boy with the broken arm. You were here when

162

Mont called the next day. You even talked to him about it.'

'You didn't tell me he was there all night. Why?'

'He wasn't.' She did not know why herself, except that she had wanted to guard the sad little disclosure of Mont's heart. 'How did Dorothy know anyway?'

'Sybil told her. She woke and heard you saying goodbye to him. So you see, you can't blame Dorothy entirely. Sybil was out to make trouble too.'

Jess got up and went quickly across the rug, which tangled the feet like poodle fur, and knelt down in front of Laurie with her arms on his knees.

'What's happened to you? How can you believe these things of people you love?' She raised her head and looked at him. His spare young face was set and hard in a way she never saw it. His mouth looked as if it would never smile again.

'It all adds up, you see,' he said drearily. 'I wanted to be there for Sybil's birthday, but you persuaded me to stay home. You worked quite hard at it, insisting that I go to the bloody dinner.'

'You had to go. You didn't want to go to Sybil's. I was trying to be nice to you.'

'Yeah.' He thought for a moment and then said: 'Dorothy said you called Mont as soon as you arrived, to ask him to come over.'

'You told me to! I didn't get him anyway, but it was your idea. Call Mont, you said. You told me to!'

But he would neither remember nor listen to her. The poison had gone into him and he was feeding on it, as it fed on him and made him a stranger.

The only time he was himself for a moment on that terrible evening was when Jess asked him, when they were in bed, cold and miserable and not touching: 'Why did you pretend at first that it was Sybil who told you all those lies?'

He did not answer for a long time. Then he gasped as if it was hard to get his breath, and said: 'I was ashamed of listening to Dorothy.' He turned away from her, and she thought that he was crying.

13

Jess had gone to England to visit her family.

'Less than a year married, and runs home to mother so soon?' Dorothy asked, with a gruesome twinkle.

'She hasn't run home.' Laurie tried to stay polite. 'She wants to see them, and this is the cheap fare season, and later she'll be too far on with the baby.'

'In my day,' Dorothy said, 'wives stayed close to their husbands when they were carrying.'

'In your day,' Laurie said rudely, 'women wouldn't let their husbands sleep with them when they were pregnant, so they had to stick around to see no one else moved in.'

Dorothy bridled, but Sybil let out a guffaw. It was the sort of remark she could still enjoy, but with which people seldom favoured her, as if her memory had gone about that too.

While Jess was away, Laurie only came once or twice to see his grandmother. He did not stay long, and seemed nervous and irritable. They were working him too hard, driving him like a nervous horse. Sybil had seen him like this before when he was at college, plunging exhausted into combat with his final exams.

At Easter, when she thought he would come, and bring her an egg with a trinket inside, he went south to stay with his mother. Sybil felt abandoned. Maud Owens was in Europe. Even the milkman had gone to Florida, and committed his deliveries to a pitted high-school boy who forgot the yoghurt.

Sybil was deserted. She did not know when Laurie would be home. Jess did not say when she was coming back. Since the day when Dorothy had forced Sybil to tell her something she did not want to tell—Sybil could not now remember what it was—she had been growing increasingly tyrannical. She was happy, singing penseroso songs like *Pale Hands I Love*, with only a sketchy idea of the words, but it was the happiness of triumph. Sometimes Sybil thought she might be drunk, even at ten o'clock in the morning. She made lines on the bottles, so that she could check, but Dorothy was not on liquor. She was intoxicated with power. She had Sybil just where she wanted her, and there was nothing that Sybil could do, for her only hope was to keep her in a good mood.

She felt that Dorothy was watching her. That was why she was not drinking: to keep a clear head. Watching and waiting. For what? For Sybil to die? One morning, her tea tasted funny. So that was it. Dorothy was slowly poisoning her. The next day, Sybil set her alarm and got up early and made the tea herself. It still tasted funny, but Dorothy drank it without comment.

Not the tea then. Something else. Sybil began to leave untouched any food that Dorothy did not eat too. But she began to feel so ill and weak that she asked Montgomery to come in and overhaul her.

'Fit as a fiddle,' he pronounced, too blithely. 'You're a remarkable woman for your age, my dear.'

'She's trying to poison me,' Sybil croaked, watching the door.

'Rats,' said Montgomery. 'I'm forced to say she's taking very fine care of you. You're in good shape.'

'Why do I feel so rotten all the time?'

'I do too.' (Nothing so maddening as a doctor who dismissed your ills by claiming them for himself.) 'It's the spring. I'll have a tonic made up for you.'

But Dorothy poured the medicine away down the sink, and gave Sybil a brew of crushed alfalfa.

Mercifully, the telephone rang. Quick as a flash when she was out of the room, Sybil poured the green mess into the calceolaria, rampaging fleshily, like all Dorothy's house plants.

Sybil wrote to Jess: *Please come back soon. I am afraid...*

A week later, she found the letter in the car when she opened the glove compartment to look for a peppermint.

'Why didn't you mail this?'

'Mercy, I forgot it. Give it me. I'll swing by the post office and mail it now.'

As she handed over the blue airmail letter, Sybil saw that it had been opened.

'You never stick your letters down properly.' Dorothy put out her mauve tongue and licked the flap.

By the time they reached the post office, Sybil had shifted forward in her seat and had her hand on the door handle. 'I'll get out, Dot.'

'Aren't you cute? But what would people think, letting you run errands for me. No, lady, you sit right there and

167

rest that poor crippled leg while Dotty does the jumping around.'

'It isn't crippled,' Sybil said, but Dorothy was already out, and banging the car door with a noise like the last barrier of sound, so Sybil continued to herself: 'All the doctors said there's nothing wrong with it.'

Dorothy came out smiling, with a handful of seed catalogues and heart-broken appeals from priests in youth camps.

If I had enough nerve, Sybil thought, I'd get right out and go in there and look in the waste-basket. 'Did you mail it?'

'That's what I went in for, wasn't it?'

She did not have enough nerve.

Once, when Dorothy was making beds upstairs, Sybil went to the telephone in the kitchen and dialled Thelma's number in Philadelphia. She would disguise her voice, so as not to waste time talking to her daughter, and when Laurie came to the phone, she would say quickly: *Come home. Oh, please come home.* There would not be time for more before Dorothy came back.

With her eye on the door into the hall, she listened to the ringing. It stopped, and someone said. 'Miz Dutton's residence.'

'May I—'

Roger gave a piercing squawk, like a parrot having its throat torn out, and Sybil hung the telephone back on the wall and moved away quickly as Dorothy's feet pounded on the shallow old stairs.

In a few minutes, the telephone rang. Relief poured through Sybil like a shot of good bourbon. The maid had guessed, had recognised her voice. Had she been there last time Sybil visited?

'I'll get it.' Dorothy left Roger, now preening and chuckling, lifted the telephone and said: 'Prince Home', as if it were a funeral parlour.

'It's for you.'

Sybil took the telephone with a wild heart, gabbling a prayer to whatever God had not totally deserted her to tell her what to say. When are you coming home? At least she could say that.

It was Montgomery.

'What did *he* want?' Dorothy asked, preparing to go back upstairs now that the conversation was over.

'He wanted Laurie's address. He's going on vacation, and he wants to send him a postal card from the Virgin Isles.'

'No comment.' Dorothy smiled and went back to making up Sybil's bed like a hospital, taut as fetters across her toes.

SYBIL WAS AFRAID for her life. She was absolutely convinced now that Dorothy was out to kill her.

It was just a question of time. And Dorothy would take her time, playing with Sybil as a cat would play with a mouse still alive in a trap.

Trapped within the walls of her own house. If she wandered outside, Dorothy would hasten after her, taking her arm uncomfortably, putting a hand under her elbow at the rough spots, as if Sybil did not know every stick and

169

stone and tuffet of this land better than Dorothy knew the runnels and open pores of her own face.

She had got to be very careful. When Dorothy suggested walking to the pond, she said it was too far. That was true. Sybil could not walk very far these days, and she had not been up the hill to the nursery and the herb garden for months.

'Take you in the wheelbarrow,' jested Dorothy, determined as she was to get Sybil to the brink and push her in.

At night, the old lady lay awake long hours, telling the Nordic sagas.

I've never done anything to her. I gave her a home. I took her in and gave her a home when she hadn't a friend in the world to turn to. They've all gone away. When you're old and ugly and you can't remember what day it is, everyone goes away.

'What does it feel like to be so old?' That girl of John's, ridiculous name, why should I remember it? I told her. I said, it feels like when you see your hostess wondering why you don't go home, so she can do the dishes. She laughed. I could always make people laugh. Syb's my clown, Papa said. When you're old and silly, they look as surprised if you cut a good joke as if the corpse sat up and spat in their eye.

Monotonously, defensively, she put the words out onto the darkness, watching the door. She would have locked the door, but Dorothy had taken away the key. Or had the key gone years before? So many people had messed around in this house that was only Sybil's, it was too much bother to remember.

When in spite of herself, she grew drowsy, she knew then for certain that Dorothy had drugged her bedtime milk.

'I don't want milk tonight,' she said, the evening after she found that out.

'Oh come, Sybilla. I just got through fixing it.' Dorothy sat her down at the table and urged the china mug on her, and Roger said: 'Drink up Sybil drink up. Sybil Sybil Sybil.'

That night, she climbed out of bed after Dorothy had gone to her room, and wedged a chair under the door handle, as they did in thrillers.

She fell asleep, and when she woke for one of the bathroom trips that were as mindless as sleepwalking, she had forgotten about the chair. She fell over it and made such a racket that Dorothy popped out of Emerson's room in a long stiff Mrs Noah dressing gown and cried: 'Dear heaven, I thought the other leg had gone at last!'

'What if it did?' Sybil asked, still vague with sleep and shock, scarcely knowing what she said. 'Would you be glad?'

'My dear little friend,' Dorothy said, most tenderly. 'Don't you know that I love you more than any person in the whole world?'

'You do?' Sybil was sitting on the chair, breathing heavily.

'Don't you know that by now? Why, I'd offer my life for you, Sybil Camden Prince, if I was ever called upon to make that gift.'

And all next day, she was as sweet and gay as only Dot could be. Cooking up special dishes in such a doting way that Sybil ate them without fear. Getting out the cards and telling Sybil's fortune. 'Long life and great prosperity. What's this, what's this? Is that a man I see looming on the horizon?'

Cackles of easy-going, familiar laughter, and a coughing

171

fit, and Roger calling for the paper boy, soup and sandwich, naughty Loll, in a frenzy of jealousy.

They went for a drive along the sea. They bought a flowered spring hat for Sybil, which made her look like a carnival horse. In the evening, they watched the late movie, and had hot toddies, and Dorothy cast on a cardigan in marbled wool, which was to be for 'my secret pal'. She winked, and laid a knitting needle alongside her nose.

Silly old secret pal. Crazy old relic. It had all been in her head. She must never admit how fearful she had been, for they would think her even farther gone than she was.

Dorothy was very charming all next day as well, so that it was a shock great enough to stop the heart when Sybil once more found her mother upstairs, wearing the brown costume, the feathered hat, the face—the face a twisted horror mask that Laurie had brought last Halloween.

Behind her, Dorothy's rasping chuckle. 'Ain't she a character?'

'Why do you do this?' Sybil asked, turning to confront her with burning eyes.

'When I was a kid, we always played dressing up. I'm a push-over for dressing up, you know.'

'But why—why—' Sybil pointed at the dummy, mute, paralysed, twisted like a stroke victim in the dim light at the top of the stairs.

'You don't think I'd presume to put your sacred mother's clothes on me? Whatever they say about me, I know my place.'

Dorothy went into her room and shut the door.

In the night, Sybil could not leave her room, because of the dummy standing guard outside. Guilty, ashamed, feeling one step nearer to that place where the old ladies sat on the commode, she took out the pretty flowered china receptacle that had been part of her bedroom set in the days before Papa had the plumbing put in.

Dorothy would be hopping mad. Well, Sybil would deny her that pleasure. She emptied it out of the window and went back to bed.

She woke again later, and heard soft footsteps in the hall. Lying very still, she could hear someone breathing outside her door.

Dawn was in the room. She watched the handle turn. The door did not open. If she were to get out of bed and put her eye to the empty keyhole, she knew that she would see another eye, gibbous, glistening. Or would it be the hollow eye of the mask, with Bella's dead eye beyond, turned up into the skull?

Sybil lay like stone, as if she were on her own tomb, and listened to her heart. She could see it thudding under the chicken bones and skin that used to be her breast. All at once, she thought of Theo. She prayed to him: Help me, dearest, although it was always she who had helped him.

It seemed an eternity before the handle turned back again, and the shuffling steps went secretly away.

So that was it. At least now I know. The poison didn't work. Now she is going to frighten me to death.

DOROTHY GRUE WAS sick. She had a sore throat, and although she refused to take her temperature, she was flushed up one minute, the network of her cheeks on fire, and the next, her teeth were chattering like bones, although they really fitted quite well. The heating system was stop and go all day, like the way she drove in traffic, from the amount of times she swivelled the thermostat impatiently back and forth.

'Why don't you go to bed, Dot dear?' Sybil suggested, after she found her vomiting raucously into the potato peelings in the sink basket.

'Never sick nor sorry,' Dorothy said without conviction. She wiped her mouth on the back of her hand. 'But I do feel a bit low, Syb. Maybe I will lie down for a while, if you're sure you'll be all right.'

'Me? There's nothing wrong with me.'

'Why else do you suppose I've fought to stay on my feet all day?' Dorothy asked piteously, thus charging Sybil neatly with whatever consequences might come of her own stubbornness.

She unhooked Roger and took him upstairs. Sybil spent an hour pottering and fiddling and weaving aimlessly back and forth between sink and stove and refrigerator, and achieved a tray of supper for Dorothy of which she was as proud as a banquet.

Chicken soup, little finger sandwiches, ice tinkling in a glass of orange juice. Who can say useless old person now? I shall take care of Dorothy, and she will know how clever and able I am, and how much she needs me. She thinks I need her. Well, now we shall see.

But all we saw was Dorothy putting a tousled black head round the door at Sybil's knock and asking how a person was supposed to eat supper when they were coughing their lungs up like a gas victim of World War One.

She did not ask it angrily. She asked it quite reasonably and patiently. Too patiently. As if the impressive feat of

174

preparing a tray supper had not altered one jot her opinion of Sybil's senility.

'Shall I bring you some milk later?' Sybil was still gasping from the climb upstairs with the tray.

'I may be asleep. If I live so long.'

'But if you're not?'

'You can leave it outside the door.'

In all the time that Dorothy had been here, Sybil had never been in her room. No invitation for a tour of the ornaments and family photographs. She had no idea what Dorothy had done with Emerson's room. She could be sleeping on spikes or printing counterfeit dollars for all she knew. When Dorothy was downstairs, the door was locked. Sybil had tried it once or twice.

She took the tray back to the kitchen, and ate the supper herself. The soup was cold, but she could not raise the spirit to put it back on the stove. She was lonely. She wandered, watched the television without registering what was on the screen, looked at pictures of smashed and twisted cars in the newspaper. She had thought it would be nice to be on her own for once, but it was impossible to settle. She wanted to ask Dorothy: Which programme? Which book? Where are my nail scissors, my glasses, my slippers? The things she had lost in these last few months! They walked off on their own, just as if they too had got sick of her, sick of belonging to somebody who forgot where she put them and then did not really care if they were lost.

By the time she was ninety, she would be living in a barren shack, uncluttered, with a spoon tied around her neck and her name on a label.

With no Roger to tell her when it was time for bed, she dozed off in front of the television, and woke hours later when all the programmes were finished and only the President and Old Glory keeping the screen.

Stumbling and mumbling, she warmed up some milk and left it outside the door with skin already forming and said: 'There you are, Mother,' loud enough for her to hear if she was awake, but not too loud to wake her if she was asleep.

'Don't make over her, Miss Sybil,' Polly had said in the kitchen, unkindly. 'It's you has had the greater loss, pet.'

Bella locked herself in her room after Papa's funeral, and then came downstairs in a blazing temper and criticised everything that had been done. Polly gave notice again—it was her way of getting a few weeks' vacation—and Sybil did the cooking. I cried into the meringue, she remembered, sitting on the edge of her bed next morning open mouthed with her stocking half-way up her good leg, arrested by a vision of the past more clear than she had enjoyed for a long time.

She took such a long time dressing that Dorothy opened her door and yelled healthily: 'What does a sick person do to get a bite of breakfast around here?'

'Oh hullo, Dot. Aren't you better then?'

'If you call having a golf ball on each side of my throat, and an iron band round my head like medieval torture being better, then yes, I am better. Thank you.'

She was wearing her long stiff dressing gown with the buttons like giant raspberries arching down the front and the hem standing on the floor all round, so that if her feet had dropped off in the night, you would never know it. Sybil had never seen her in pyjamas. She knew that Dorothy wore pyjamas, because she had seen them on the line, square, short-legged, slapping at the wind.

'I'm so sorry, Dot. Have you tried your pills?'

176

'The box is empty. I want you to bring me up some more.' Dorothy had not combed her dry black hair, but she had put on lipstick. She always put on lipstick as soon as she woke up, or else she went to bed in it. There was a stain of it on her teeth, carnivorous.

'Of course, dear.' Good, she was needed again. 'I'll bring them up with your breakfast.'

But when she looked in the cupboard where they kept the herbal remedies, the jar where Dorothy stored the parsnip and bilberry pills that stood between her and lung cancer was empty.

What to do? Make some more? I could. I'll bet I could. But it would take time. Tell her first? Get breakfast? Start the pills?

In a confusion of indecision, Sybil bumped round the kitchen, picking things up and putting them aimlessly down, pouring prune juice and spilling it, bending with a groan to get out the old wooden mixing bowl, starting for the stairs and coming back again, for if she reported no pills, Dorothy would be angry. She would set the cords of her neck and pull her lips back, and Sybil would see the lipstick on her teeth.

'Sybil!'

Well, she was angry now anyway, so there it was. Sybil went to the foot of the stairs and looked up. Dorothy was standing over the stair-well, hands gripping the rail, face scarlet as she leaned forward in a paroxysm of painful coughing.

'Where are my pills?' she croaked. She leaned over Sybil with her red face and her bulging eyes, and Sybil thought that she would fall on her and smother her with the crimson robe, the wooden raspberry buttons biting into her face.

'There aren't any.'

'Dear God alive,' said Dorothy in a towering rage, although it was she who had eaten the pills. 'So now you expect me to drag myself down there and mix up some more.'

'I'm sorry, Dot.' Sybil stood at the bottom of the stairs forlornly, with her eyes turned up to the heaving scarlet pouter breast, the staring, pitiless eyes.

'I'm coming down.' It sounded like a threat.

THAT EVENING, DOROTHY was dead. Sybil knew that she was dead, because although she was lying there on the bed with her eyes open, she did not say a word when Sybil went to the dressing-table and picked up a photograph in an ornate gilt frame of a lot of grown-ups and children with faces like pigs standing round a wheelchair where an ancient baby glowered.

She picked it right up and held it near her eyes because she had not been able to find her glasses for days, and examined it closely before deciding that the pig in the billowing shirtwaist was Dorothy, centuries ago. She put it down again, with all those ugly faces to the wall.

'Hullo Sybil.'

She turned in a flash, the blood running out of her like an emptied bath so that her feet were lead, rooted, and her head swayed empty and dizzy.

Roger was in his domed cage on a table near the bed, regarding her sideways with his papery seed-shaped eye. Dorothy was still lying there with her eyes rolled back, her jaw dropped, and the top half of her teeth dropped with it across the cavern of her mouth.

Get her teeth in, quick Bridget.

When Sybil was in the hospital, a young nurse had come flying in with her hair all at odds, and cried to the older nurse who was dressing Sybil's leg: 'Mrs McKenzie's gone!'

'Get her teeth in, Bridget. If you leave it, you'll never get 'em in.'

So Sybil went over to the bed where she had so often made Emerson lie and breathe for her, and tried to push Dorothy's top teeth back against her gums. It seemed like a liberty, especially as Dorothy had always preserved the fiction of: Thank goodness I've still got all my teeth, but she was dead now, and dethroned.

Another of the fictions had been: 'I'm happy to say I haven't a grey hair.' Bending closer now, touching the clammy skin with curious, daring fingertips, trying to turn the head on the stiffening neck, Sybil saw that the roots of the dead black hair were coming in snow white.

'You should have thought of that before you died, and given yourself a treatment,' Sybil told her in a school-mistressy voice.

After a while, if Dorothy went on lying there and could not use the colouring bottle, her hair would all be quite white, and she would look as old as Sybil.

'You don't look like any young girl now, Dot, I'll tell you that,' Sybil said. Her voice sounded weird in the empty room. Roger was silent, scrabbling under his wing as if he had lice, and then shaking himself up into a ruffled ball and letting the plumage gradually subside into sleekness before he started all over again, scrabbling and ruffling.

It was no wonder that Dorothy was not looking her best, for she had had a rough passage that day. The first time Sybil ventured into the room, emboldened by her cries for help, she was vomiting all over everything, and doubled up with her hands over her stomach, screaming that somebody was slicing her in two.

'Oh dear, poor Dot.' Sybil went down to look in the herbal to see what was good for that, but she could not read the small precise writing of her ancestor. She looked in the herb remedy cupboard aimlessly, ran a few plates under the tap, and then sat drumming her fingers at the table, wondering what day of the week it was, and why she was there, and what life was all about in any case.

Whisky, that was the thing. Dot liked her glass— well, don't we all? She poured a stiff shot of bourbon, made a new pencil mark on the bottle, and climbed upstairs to Emerson's door.

'May I come in?'

A groan.

Sybil opened the door cautiously. Dorothy was still on the bed. Her face was green and blue, like Danish cheese, and she was groaning faintly with each expiration.

'Here's for what ails you!' Sybil said brightly, fancying herself as a bustling nurse-figure. She would have to look out her old sneakers. 'This will hit the spot.'

That was what Dorothy said when she gave Sybil fearsome concoctions like the sour wine and willow leaves. But this was the best bourbon. Old Somebody-or-other— Grandpa, Uncle, Cousin—they gave them these names.

'Drink up Sybil Sybil,' the bird said when he saw her hold out the glass.

'No, this is for your mother,' Sybil told him.

Dorothy shook her head feebly. 'I can't move my arms.'

'You're just weak. Here, Sybil will help you. Trust old Syb. You can depend on good old Sybilla. You can be sure if it's Westinghouse.' Keep cheerful, that was it. She put down the glass, and with a superhuman effort, pulled Dorothy forward a little and propped the pillows behind her.

'No—' she protested, as Sybil picked up the glass again, but Sybil said: 'Naughty, naughty,' and as an afterthought picked up a few of the mud coloured cough pills from the open box and popped them into Dorothy's mouth before she poured in a drench of whisky that made Dorothy gasp and choke and retch. But she swallowed, her eyes streaming, and Sybil forced in another pill for good measure, and another swallow of liquor to wash it down, and left her.

It was a pity that Dorothy had vomited so much. All that good bourbon. When Sybil came back later, she looked as if she were in some kind of a fit, putting it on most likely, to get attention. There was too much mess to clean up, so Sybil put sheets of newspaper down over the worst places in Marma's hooked rug, and got a clean sheet from the linen closet and spread that over the rigid body, which seemed to be locked in some kind of conflict with itself.

A doctor? The thought of Montgomery flitted through her mind, his long bony limbs spreadeagled on some faraway tropic beach. But Dorothy would never see him, even if he flew straight to her in his swimming trunks. She would not let any doctor into her room. Even old Matson with his mumbling and grumbling and his: 'That gall-bladder should have come out years ago.'

Sybil stayed upstairs and turned out her handkerchief drawer and her purse drawer, so as to be nearby in case she was needed. But she might as well be dead as far as Dorothy was concerned. There was no sound from the room, and when Sybil went back in there late that after-noon—how bold she was getting, popping in and out just as if it were any room in the house!—Dorothy seemed to be asleep. You could not hear her breathing. The mound of sheet that was her bosom did not seem to move at all, and although her eyes were open, they stared blankly when Sybil stood before her in the failing light.

Sybil put out a finger and touched her cheek. It was clammy like a toad. She went into Dorothy's old bedroom over the side porch to fetch a blanket, forgot what she had gone for, and became interested in the fat chestnut buds unfolding just outside the window.

When she went back eventually with the Mexican blanket that Theo had brought back from somewhere or other—Mexico?—Dorothy did not wake when she laid it tenderly over her. Sybil switched on the light, and Roger began to chirp and mutter, as he always did when a room was lit up. Still no news from Emerson's bed. It was then that Sybil picked up the family photograph, knocking a jar of face cream to the floor, and knew that Dorothy was dead, because she just lay there and did not say a word.

In the days that followed these strange events, Sybil veered between being lucid and quite confused.

When she was confused, she could not remember what had happened to Dorothy. She expected to see her in every room she went into, stirring gravy, bending hippily to lay the fire, polishing a table with a hand fat and purple from the pressure she put into it. When she went into the front room upstairs to feed Roger, or to kneel at the window in a luxury of hate for the cars, it was quite a surprise to find Dorothy still there on the bed, looking a little worse each day and smelling, let's face it, Dot, terrible.

When her head was clear, she knew quite well that Dorothy was dead. But there it was. Nothing could be done. Inscrutable are Thy purposes, Lord.

The morning after she died, Anna Romiza arrived and found Sybil in the kitchen brewing a cup of instant tea, which she had always pretended to Dorothy was an offence against the traditions of her English ancestry, but which she really rather liked.

'Where Miz Grue then?' Anna's broad, dark-fleshed face with the magenta mouth spread all over the bottom of it was a comfort to see. Sybil realised that she had been very much alone for hours. Had she been to bed? She could not remember. Her skirt looked somewhat wrinkled. She might well have slept in it.

She was on the point of telling Anna that Dorothy was dead, for Anna would know what to do, since she spent as much time visiting people in funeral homes as other women spend having coffee with the neighbours, when she was arrested by an extremely clear vision, like a sign from heaven, of that flat old lady with the rails around her bed as if she were a wild beast.

With Dorothy dead, that's where Sybil would go. They

183

had taken her there to show her what would happen if she did not behave. They had taken her there to try and trap her into being crazy enough to be locked up for good.

'She's sick, Anna,' she said casually. 'She'll have to stay in bed for a while.'

'That's too bad.' Anna started for the stairs. 'I'll go up and see if there's anything she wants.'

'Oh no.' Sybil jumped up with an agility that surprised herself, and put a hand on Anna's muscular arm. 'She doesn't want to be disturbed. She told me. I don't believe you'd better go upstairs at all, Anna. We can let the cleaning go up there just for now.'

'You're the boss.' Anna said cheerfully. She did not like hauling the bulky old vacuum cleaner upstairs any better than she liked the idea of waiting on Dorothy.

'Sybil Sybil Sybil.'

As she opened the door of Emerson's room, she half expected to see Dorothy sitting up in bed, demanding bran flakes and rose-hip syrup, but it was Roger, carrying on like a madman in his cage, with a stream of incoherent comment about Roger Grue and double double toil and trouble, which was what Dorothy always said when she stirred decoctions on Priscilla.

'What's the matter with you?' Sybil asked him crossly, for he had startled her, which everyone knew was not good for her. 'Do you want to go out?'

The bedroom window was shut. Dorothy had never thought much of the night air. Feeling clever, Sybil bent to check that the damper was across the chimney, and then opened the door of the bird cage.

Roger flew to the top of one of the bare posts at the head of the bed and stayed there. He stayed there all day,

184

clutching its rounded top with curved claws, while Dorothy lay silent below, and Sybil fancied that her hair was growing, for when she lit the bedside lamp, she thought she could see more white coming in at the roots.

Anna had made lunch for her, and had left her something to heat up in the oven for her supper.

'What about Miz Grue?' she asked before she left. She despised Dorothy, but she was not going to see the poor woman starve to death.

'I'm taking her up some soup.' Sybil took a can at random from the cupboard, opened it, and began to heat it on the stove.

'You better dilute it with water,' Anna said, watching her narrowly.

'Of course, ha ha, how silly of me.' Sybil took the saucepan to the tap and splashed in what she guessed was the right amount, for she had thrown the can away.

'You sure you going to be O.K.?' Anna was still standing by the door in her mauve coat and her shoes, her working slippers in her hand.

'Of course. Don't fuss.'

'I'll come by tomorrow.'

'It's not your day.'

'Every day going to be my day till that woman gets up to take care of you.'

So Anna came every day, and cooked for Sybil and did the marketing, and brought in what little mail there was. A letter from Jess. 'My mother sends her best wishes. They are saving money to come over to the States for a visit.'

Well, I don't want them.

A postcard from Laurie, with a picture of a hotel

like a jail. He had gone to Florida with a friend.

A letter from Montgomery, but Sybil could not read his handwriting.

A few bills, which she put on a spike for Laurie.

When she realised, because of the bills, that it must be the end of the month, she wrote out Dorothy's cheque and put it in an envelope, stamped it and gave it to Anna to mail on her way home.

Anna brought it back the next day without comment from Sybil's box at the post office, and Sybil took it upstairs and laid it on Dorothy's dressing table.

'Sybil Sybil Sybil.' That was about all the bird would say these days, he was not much use as company. He stayed in Emerson's room most of the time, but if Sybil left the door open to air the place out a bit after Anna had gone home, he would fly out and perch on the banisters to call to Sybil if she was downstairs.

'What is it?' she would call back. But he would never say. One morning, he called so loudly from a picture frame in the hall that the milkman heard him.

'Her ladyship wants you.' He winked, brown and handsome from his surfing holiday. The milkman had not liked Dorothy since she told him that his orange juice curdled even quicker than his milk. She was like that with the tradespeople. Always too sharp. Alienating local friends whom Sybil had known since they were tiny bullet-headed boys dressed up in sheets, mewing at her door for Halloween candy.

'Sybil,' Roger said again, and coughed.

'How is she?' the milkman asked, not even simulating concern.

'A little better, thank you. I'm keeping her very quiet.' She shut the door almost in his charming face, for if

Dorothy was calling her, she had to get up there double quick, dot and carry or no.

Some days she grew confused between Roger and Dorothy. Some days she knew it was Dorothy on the bed and Roger on the bedpost. Some days she talked to Dorothy for long spells at a time, and it seemed that Dorothy answered in her head. Is that so? she said, and: You've told me that anecdote before, lady. How about putting on another record?

Some days it seemed that Dorothy was there, her presence everywhere in the house, with a chance of meeting her around every corner. Some days it seemed that she was gone for good, and Sybil would rove freely through the house, calling out dreadful things about her, and sticking out her tongue at the snapshot of Dorothy in her high red boots in the snow, which curled in the frame of the sitting-room mirror.

She spent quite a lot of time in Emerson's room, pottering, fiddling, looking at everything Dorothy had. What a pretty pocket-book! She took it off to her own room, gay bouquets of flowers on a little basket, and put it on her purse shelf, where it looked surprisingly at home. Why shouldn't it? It was her pocket-book that Jess bought for her at Bonwits last summer.

She found her nail scissors with the stork blades in a drawer with a mess of old lipsticks and cracking rouge. She found her reading glasses on the closet shelf, wrapped in pink face tissue.

Sometimes, Dot, you carry a joke too far. She wrinkled her nose. If she could have caught Roger and put him back in his cage, she would have opened the window, but he had been free since she let him out.

It was a good thing Dorothy had lost her sense of smell,

187

Sybil thought dottily, shutting Emerson's door and going downstairs with her head feeling light as a dandelion ball, or she could never have lived with it.

On one of her meanderings through the house, enjoying her freedom, still half expecting to hear: 'What are you up to now—you'll trip and fall again,' Sybil wandered into Ted's room and saw Bella's dummy, naked and headless, pushed carelessly among the litter of picnic baskets and dusty dress boxes at the end of the narrow room.

Poor Marma. There's not much respect for the dead.

Sybil stood the dummy upright. The waist was quaintly small, but the bosom was noble and dominating. It looked a bit like old Dot, to tell the truth. How would it look in that navy dress with all the gilt buttons running down the front like a Guardee?

Dorothy liked dressing up. Here was something she could enjoy, bad shape as she was in. Puffing and uttering the small oaths that came quite often to her lips now that there was nobody to hear, Sybil got hold of the dummy by the neck and dragged it through to the other part of the house, its wooden stand bumping and scraping on the uneven floorboards.

She took it into Emerson's room and stood it in the hollow in the middle of the floor, and dressed it up in Dorothy's new outfit, with two towels stuffed in the front to take up the slack. Headless, it did not look much. What was it Dorothy had done in the days when she was trying to frighten Sybil to death?

Dorothy's Easter bonnet was in a box on a high shelf. Sybil knocked it down, bringing with it a pile of shoe boxes and a beach hat that said Cape Cod, Mass. The Easter hat was a flowerpot in full bloom. Ridiculously young, Sybil had thought at the time, but Dorothy was headstrong about hats, making that dead set face in the mirror at the store that made the hat look even less suitable than it was.

It nested in tissue paper. Sybil wadded that up and balanced it on the dummy's wooden neck, with the flowerpot hat on top.

'There you are Dot,' she said, either to the dummy or the body, it did not matter which, 'in all your glory. I do try to please you, you see. Never say I don't try to do anything to please you.'

14

'LET'S SURPRISE HER!'

Jess came back to America sooner than she had planned. Laurie came home before his three weeks' vacation was over.

'I couldn't stay away from you,' Jess said immediately at the airport, searching his triangular brown face.

'Forgive me.'

'There's nothing to forgive.'

'I never really believed—'

' I know you didn't'

'Why did you go away?'

'I had to.'

'You never will again.'

They clung, in the arrival hall, while crowds pushed round them, and unlikely people, squat, deprived, rushed at unlikely people who had been on the plane with Jess.

The apartment across the Charles River was home, like a shell. Her mother's house had been as strange as a hotel, but more uncomfortable. Soon they must move. The lease was due, and this would be too small with the baby. They would never again live in a small cave, alone. There would be the suburbs, a garden, bunk beds for all their boys, white machines churning endlessly at her control in the cellar.

Without telephoning Sybil, they went to Plymouth to surprise her.

'Poor old lady,' Laurie said, as they turned off the highway and up onto the bridge to get across to the yellow house. 'Won't she be glad to see us!'

'We're so egotistical,' Jess said happily. 'She's probably hardly noticed we've been away.'

And indeed, when they came calling through the door and found Sybil sitting idle in the half dark, she did not seem unduly surprised.

'Glad you could make it,' she said, as if it were just an ordinary weekend.

'What's the matter, Gramma?' Laurie switched on the light and then stood in front of her, frowning. 'Have you been sick?'

'I've been fine.' But she looked dreadful, bony and yellow, her eyes sunk in red hollows. Her hair was wild, and she had odd clothes thrown on at random. Her skirt was back to front and her shoes did not match.

'Where's Dorothy?'

'She's sick.'

'Why didn't you let us know?'

'Oh—it hasn't been for long. I've been all right.'

'Who's been looking after you?'

'Anna comes every day. She's been very kind, though I must confess I'm getting a little tired of pork chops.'

'Where's Dorothy?'

'Upstairs in her room.'

Jess heard Sybil cry: 'No!' as she started up the stairs.

191

Before she reached the top, the stench hit her and she called out, and in a moment, Laurie was behind her.

They went into Emerson's room together, hand in hand, staring, for some reason, as Jess remembered afterwards, on tiptoe.

They saw the dummy in the flowered hat, and then they saw the bed.

WHEN THE MEDICAL EXAMINER asked Sybil: 'Why, Mrs Prince? Why didn't you tell anyone?' she would not answer. She hung her head like a child, and started to cry.

'Leave her alone,' Laurie said. 'It's bad enough for her, without being cross examined.'

'She may have to answer a cross examination in court,' the Medical Examiner said, 'if the District Attorney decides on an inquest.'

But he was a blue jay squawking drama, hoping to give evidence in court himself. There would be no inquest, since it was all too clear that Dorothy had poisoned herself by mistake with the powdered root of the false hellebore which she kept as an insecticide for her roses. Pathological examination after the autopsy revealed powerful toxic alkaloids, which had probably caused convulsions, paralysis, and finally death from asphyxia.

'Asphyxia, don't tell me,' stormed Dorothy's sister,

who arrived, as well she might, in a fierce state of affront which became fiercer when she was told that she could not view the body.

'It's not—well, surely you would rather remember Dorothy as you knew her,' Jess said, trying hard, for although she disliked Mrs Hubbard on sight, she was, after all, the dead woman's sister.

'There's something funny going on around here,' Mrs Hubbard said, and Laurie poured her a huge dry martini, which she first refused, and then drank like water.

'It's terribly sad,' Jess said. 'We're all very upset about it, naturally.'

'Naturally, since now you don't have anyone to do your duty for you, taking care of the old lady.'

'Now listen—' Laurie took a step forward, but Jess shook her head at him.

'Dorothy was happy here,' she said evenly—it was much easier to keep calm when you were pregnant. 'We were all very fond of her.'

'You had the radio on when I arrived. Don't deny it. I heard it through the door.' The sister was smaller than Dorothy, but she had the same never-bested air that caused both condolences and explanations to slip off her like oil on a griddle.

'Well, gosh,' Jess said, 'you can't expect us to sit round crying all day. I mean, we're dreadfully sorry, but that wouldn't help Dorothy now, would it?'

'The help should have come before it was too late,' Mrs Hubbard said, striving to get her lips over her long shiny teeth.

'But we were away, and my husband's grandmother— how was she to know that Dorothy had made the pills up with the wrong powder? She didn't know one from the

193

other. She never went up to the shed where the storage jars were kept. She can't walk that far.'

'Apart from the rights and wrongs of messing around with those so-called herbal remedies, which my sister would never have thought of if she hadn't come to this unlucky house, I can't believe she could make that kind of mistake.'

Laurie tipped the martini jug over her glass, and she glared at him and drank it, her teeth showing inside the glass as she tilted it back for the olive.

'It must have been because she wasn't well,' Jess said. 'She mixed up the powders. Hellebore, for rose spray. Veratrum viride, the chemist called it. I'd show you the rest of the jar, only they took it away.'

'There's something funny about the whole thing,' Dorothy's sister repeated, but with less conviction than before the gin. She would have thought it funnier still if she had known that Dorothy had lain dead in the front bedroom at Camden House for more than a week. Nobody knew that except Laurie and Jess and the doctors, and it had been kept out of the newspapers.

Sybil came into the room, leaning heavily on her stick, and bowed with distant courtesy to Dorothy's sister.

'It's a pleasure to see you again, Mrs Prince.' Mrs Hubbard got up, but put her hands behind her back to make it clear that the pleasure did not extend to shaking hands.

'Have we met?'

'Why does she pretend not to remember me? I've been here before. She took me over the whole house. You see— there is something funny going on.'

'What nonsense,' Jess said, angered now because Sybil looked so battered and bewildered. 'Of course she remem-

bers you. You remember Dorothy's sister from Provincetown, don't you, Gramma?'

'I didn't even know Dot had a sister,' Sybil said,
pleasantly enough.

The Medical Examiner came again, as a formality
because Mrs Hubbard asked him to, and ate cucumber
sandwiches with the plump white hands that had delved
into the secrets of Dorothy. When he asked Sybil once
more, also as a formality, since he had written her off as
quite senile, why she had kept Dorothy upstairs for so
long, she shook her head and looked at him as if he were
talking Arabic.

'Mother dear,' said Laurie's mother, who had come up
from Philadelphia to find out, as she said, what the hell
was going on, since she could make nothing of her son's
gabble on the telephone, 'you've forgotten to feed your
cats. They are lined up in the kitchen as if they were waiting to shake hands with the Governor.'

When Sybil had left the room, Thelma asked the bald
square doctor: 'What do you think we should do? What's
your opinion of her? She has no family physician now that
Dr Matson has retired.'

'She does. She has Montgomery. Doctor Jones.'

'Oh, that young man,' said Thelma, and the Medical
Examiner said: 'Doctor Jones, yes. Quite an able young
fellow. But he's away now, I think.'

'Let's wait till he comes back,' Laurie said to his
mother, 'and then have him look at Gramma. She seems
all right now. I know what she did was a bit off, but she
seems to have forgotten all about it, and she's been perfectly normal since we came. Better than ever. She goes in
cycles, you know. One week she's not making much sense,
and the next, she's just like her old self.'

'You don't need to explain her to me.' Thelma raised her eyebrows, which she had plucked too recklessly and pencilled back in. 'She is my mother, after all, not yours.'

'But you,' said Laurie, who was always polite to his mother, even under stress, 'haven't seen nearly as much of her as Jess and I have.'

'From your own choice,' snapped Thelma. 'Remember that, Laurie. Nobody has ever asked you to fawn around.'

'I'll have to be going.' The doctor spoke to Jess, since it would need a blow torch to break through the icy tension between Laurie and his mother.

'But you haven't told us what you think.' Thelma turned her back on Laurie and gave the doctor the closed lips social smile she kept for people she supposed she had better be charming to, without knowing why. 'Don't you agree that for her own sake, we ought to—'

'Mother, how can you!' Laurie said, and Jess said: 'No,' and put a hand over her mouth.

'Taunton,' said the doctor. 'Well, yes, I daresay. I can examine her myself, if you like, unless you prefer to wait for Doctor Jones. I imagine he would agree that it might be best to have her committed.'

'He never would,' Laurie said, 'and if you try to send my grandmother to a mental institution, I'll have you prosecuted.'

'That's a boy,' said the doctor equably. 'Family loyalty. I like that.'

'How could you?' Laurie rounded on his mother after the doctor had left. 'Your own mother.'

'Don't dramatise, sweetie. She is pretty far gone, after all. I mean,' she raised her eyes, 'what she did up there. If you can forget that, I can't. If you want my opinion, which I know means nothing in your arrogant young

life, she doesn't have any of her marbles. Not one.
I thought you were rather rude to that fat doctor,' she
added lightly.

'I'm not going to let him shut her up.'

'What's the alternative?'

'Find another Dorothy.'

'They don't grow on every tree. Thank God. I couldn't
stand the woman.' Thelma made the sign of the cross
backwards, to counteract speaking ill of the dead.

'We'll have to get a nurse then.'

'You know what *that* costs.'

'Well, couldn't you—'

'You forget dear. What money I had, your father
drank away. What money I have now belongs to my husband.'

'Uncle John?'

Thelma laughed. 'With two kids in college? I doubt it.
He's quite deeply in debt, I understand. No, if you won't
let the State take care of poor Mother, we shall have to
find some nice cosy nursing home within her means,
where she can have her own things and get the proper
care she needs.'

The purr in her voice drew a picture of a chintzy room,
with Sybil's ornaments and pictures and her own beloved
quilt, plants on a sunny window-sill, hymns on Sunday
afternoon, a pretty nurse laying a single flower on the
tray of chicken and jelly.

Jess and Laurie sat on the fence between the meadow
and the lawn, with the last legacy of the sun streaked
yellow and green at their backs between the pines, and
agreed that Thelma might be right.

'If she could do that, and the dummy dressed up and
everything.' Jess shivered, watching the windows of the

197

house, where Sybil was walking through drawing curtains, faithful to the memory of Dorothy Grue. 'There's no knowing what she might do next. I could go and look at that new place on the shore road. Do you think she might like it? Nothing to worry about. People to talk to—'

Sybil came out of the back door, looking for them in the dusk. 'I've lit the broiler,' she said efficiently, as Jess jumped carefully down, feeling the great weight of herself and the half-grown baby squashing the soft turf. 'I thought you'd want to start the steak. Thelma says she must go to bed early so she can leave first thing in the morning. I wonder why she came? She was asleep through most of poor Dot's memorial service. I saw her. Was it Thelma who asked that doctor to come back? If he is a doctor. I thought at first he was a plain clothes detective, since he kept asking me why I kept Dorothy upstairs for so long after she died. As if I could have moved her.'

It was the first time she had spoken about that. Jess had thought she was too confused to remember.

'Why did you, Gramma?' she asked on an impulse, taking Sybil by her thin upper arms. 'Why didn't you tell someone, when you knew that she was dead?'

'You should know why.' Sybil looked into her face, her pouched eyes drawing up towards the furrows in the middle of her brow. 'I couldn't tell, because I knew that if there was no Dot, no one to look after me, I'd have to be shut up in one of those places where they put the crazy old ladies.'

Small tears began to trickle down her cheeks and into the folds of skin at the corners of her trembling mouth. She did not bend her head nor raise a hand to her eyes. She just stood looking into Jess's face and crying feebly.

When Thelma heard that Laurie and Jess had decided

to let the rest of the lease on the Cambridge apartment go, and move into Camden House with Sybil, she said: 'You're insane. But you will do what you want, I suppose. You always have.'

Laurie would drive to and from Boston every day, and Jess would leave her job in the college admissions office, which she had planned to do soon anyway. The future? That would take care of itself. For her summer, she would take care of Laurie and Sybil and the house, and wait for her baby.

Sybil was happy, brighter and more sensible than they had known her for some time. Laurie and Jess were more deeply in love than they had ever been. Jess felt well and strong and so securely content that it was hard to imagine this house as the place of ghosts and fear which her sick imagination had made it. She was not afraid. The house seemed once more like a place that she could love as home.

Emerson's room was shut up and would not be used again, but she did not mind passing the door, even in the dark, testing herself by not turning on the light. Roger was back on his hook in the kitchen, seducing his reflection in the mirror with kissing noises and chirrups. He had not spoken a word since Dorothy was taken away, and with any luck he never would again.

Laurie had wanted to wring his neck or gas him in the oven, but Jess refused. 'It wasn't his fault.' She put a finger to his open door, but he had not been out of the cage since they caught him upstairs under a waste-basket and put him back in.

'What wasn't his fault?'

'Everything. Dorothy poisoning herself. Sybil going so queer.'

'I'm not so sure. I've never trusted that bird. If he really is the reincarnation of poor Grue's boy friend, I'd say Henry was a man who was better dead. The cats will soon fix Roger anyway.'

The cats were back. Jess had brought them down from the barn. Some of the younger ones were too wild to stay in the house, but the black panther who could make bird noises moved back in, and a striped female, and the old ginger who slept on the radiators.

Laurie bought Jess a little car, so that she would not be stranded when he was in Boston. Sybil was so active and walking so well that she took her to the replica of the first Pilgrim village, and while she was there, she found out that they were short of a guide, and went to the manager's office to ask if she could have the job.

'How much do you know about the early settlers?'

'My husband's family came over in the Mayflower.' She had not seen that as an advantage before.

'Yes, we know.' The manager laughed. He knew Sybil's family quite well. 'But the British have got so many centuries of their own history to learn, they don't get around to learning much about ours, even their own part in it.'

'I don't know much about anything,' Jess said cheerfully. 'But we have all the books at home, and I'll read it up. You can give me a test if you like.'

'We shall anyway,' the man said, 'and you'll have to take lessons from one of our senior guides on how to talk, and how to handle the public.'

'Do they riot?'

'They ask dam-fool questions, which is worse.'

One of the things they said to Jess, after she got the job and stood there in her long brown dress in the Myles

Standish house, telling the tale to all who cared to listen, was: 'But you're British!'

'So were the Pilgrims.' Her sweetest smile, docile, maidenly.

'Well, how about that? I guess you're right. Funny thing, I always thought of them as Americans.'

Anna Romiza agreed to come every afternoon to stay with Sybil while Jess was at the Pilgrim village.

'Let me see you!' Sybil always called out from her bed where she was resting when she heard Jess come out of her room, so Jess had to go and stand in the doorway in her cap and her big white collar and her dark green bodice and long brown wool skirt, so bunchy at the waist that all the guides looked pregnant, whether they were or not, so it did not matter about Jess.

'Dorothy would have liked that.' Sybil chuckled. 'Poor Dot, she always wanted to be a Pilgrim maid. She liked to brew herbs and simples, you know, like they used to. Did I tell you?'

'Yes, Gramma, you told me. I must fly. I'm late.'

Laurie took a picture of her driving off in the little sports car in her Pilgrim outfit. It looked very funny, like nuns in a station wagon. The guides were not allowed to smoke while they were driving in costume, and if the manager could have made them go to work on horseback, he would.

The village was called Plimoth Plantation, because that was the way they used to spell it. It was a street of small wooden houses with reed-thatched roofs, laid out just as the settlers had built, with a college boy on vacation firing an ancient flintlock on the fort roof, and a man in a woollen hat pushing a primitive saw philosophically back and forth in the same broad piece of timber.

The whole exhibit was so meticulously authentic that some people, already confused after seeing the Mayflower II, believed it was the original village, and touched carefully 'antiqued' beams reverently and said: 'I'll bet this could tell a tale or two.'

Jess smiled her Pilgrim smile, and did not always disillusion them, if that was what they wanted.

It was curiously peaceful, in spite of the crowds. Sometimes she felt as if she actually lived here, and would be climbing into the little wooden bed sunk in the wall after the people had gone away. The wax figures of the settlers became familiar friends. She was proud of them.

In her own family, there was no talk of ancestors, no speculation about those long dead weavers from the North, no interest in anything beyond one's own life span. The pride of Laurie's family had seemed exaggerated, difficult to share. Now she began to understand.

'We are not descended from fearful men.'

She began to understand the courage that had hacked a living here out of nothing. It had taken the English.

Once she had to go back at dusk after the village was closed to fetch something she had left behind. Shall I be afraid? But the figures were relaxed, waiting harmlessly for daylight. The boy with the toothache, the sweating surgeon about to plunge his knife into the artistic swelling on the man's leg—she patted them serenely, as if they were animals bedded down for the night, and went back up the deserted street unhurriedly, relishing her freedom from the imagery of fear.

The only place in which she felt uncomfortable was the booth with the herbal medicine exhibit, which had first started Dorothy on the road to her own destruction. Although it was outdoors in a perpetual east wind from the sea, the herbs and roots and the powders and pestles and pills evoked once more the sweet smell of death which lurked, ready to haunt Jess for ever.

When she was tired, she sat on a bench in the sun, with her round-toed shoes drawn neatly under her skirt, and added local colour, and people would stop and ask her questions, and exclaim about her English accent, sometimes with pleasure, sometimes with mild affront, as if she was cheating.

Sometimes instead of asking questions, they would give her the answers to questions that had not been asked. It was wonderful how much Americans knew about their own history, although as the manager had said, there being so little of it made it easier.

But she could not imagine her father and her mother, nor either of her brothers, stumping round Penshurst or Longleat and handing out bits of information to the guide. They had all been to Blenheim once, and her mother's ankle had turned in the courtyard, because she had insisted on wearing her 'illusion' heels, and one of her sister-in-law's children had wet on the staircase.

It was a very happy summer. Jess loved her job at Plimoth Plantation, and loved wearing the anonymous costume and being able to stand with her stomach stuck out, resting her clean Pilgrim hands modestly on the baby.

Sybil was no trouble. She was placid and content, and apart from remembering very little except stray incidents from her ancient history which bubbled inconsequentially to the surface, she was quite sensible.

She lost things all the time. Once when it was her glasses again, she said: 'Dorothy took them.'

Jess looked at her.

'I found them in her room, wrapped up and hidden.

203

She used to hide my things to make me think I was stupid. She took my glasses, and I couldn't see.'

'I'll find them.' Jess began to poke in the seats of the deep chairs. 'Dorothy isn't here now, remember.'

'No, she isn't here any more.' Sybil nodded. 'That's right, she isn't here.'

Friends began to come again almost every weekend. They swam and sailed and had great meals and great irrelevant discussions lying on the lawn in the dark after the twilight insects had gone. Some of the young men and Laurie and Montgomery cleared the tennis court, and bought a load of clay, and they were levelling it down and tearing out and rebuilding the rusted wire netting that had collapsed long ago into the arms of the ramblers.

It was like those first months when Melia Mulligan was there, and the house had been alive and alight with love and friendship, and Laurie and Jess had planned their future here, and marked out the space for their children's names on the grey prehistoric bark of the weeping beech.

Jess had been afraid of what would happen when Montgomery came back, but he and Laurie were just the same as before, the madness and the jealousy vanished as if it had never seeped in to poison their lives.

Montgomery was quite interested in a girl who was somebody's sister, a tall girl with light hair and gentle eyes, who never wore shoes and never hurried.

'She's lazy though,' Jess said, pursing her lips like her mother. 'She wouldn't make him a very good wife.'

'Mont hasn't got as far as that. He only likes her because she looks a bit like you.'

'What do you mean?'

'You know he's been in love with you for ages.'

204

'I didn't know you knew. Poor Mont, it was only because—if I had known, I would have told you he was here that night.'

'That was what hurt. You not telling me. I never really believed what she said. But then you hadn't told me, that's what I couldn't understand. And that woman, she planted the idea in me like the seed of something horrible that grew and choked me. I couldn't think straight.'

'She tried to tell me something about you too, when you weren't here. She was cunning. She didn't exactly say anything, but she hinted about why you hadn't come. I should have hit her in the mouth, plugged my ears, run away. I didn't want to listen, but I had to.'

'Why?'

'She made me. There was something about her. She made me listen, and think about it. That was the worst thing, that I was thinking about it. That was when I—' She would not tell him about the image that had hung across the bed from her, and reached out its icy hand. That was in another life, another Jess, neurotic, brooding, afraid.

'She made you. Yes, that's how it was. I wouldn't listen to her. I went away. But I had to come back. She was sitting in that chair, waiting. She knew I would come back. She made me listen to her filth.'

'Do you think she had some kind of evil spirit? Could she? Everything went wrong. Gramma went to pieces. We fought. I was so unhappy, and you were too, weren't you?'

He nodded, staring at her.

'Haven't you noticed—it seems a dreadful thing to say —but Laurie, haven't you noticed that everything began to be all right after she died?'

Involuntarily, they both glanced at the chair where

Dorothy used to sit and sip her sherry, with a fuming ashtray on her knee and the bird on the edge of the peanut bowl.

They looked back at each other, and Jess whispered: 'I'm glad she's dead.'

GOING THROUGH HER winter clothes, to see what there would be to wear after the baby was born, Jess found the letter she had written to Aunt Mary in the pocket of her grey flannel skirt, where she had pushed it, unfinished, the night Montgomery came.

Afterwards, when everything fell about her ears, and she had fled to England, she had not thought again about her cry for help to Mary.

Lucky that she had never finished the letter and sent it. Mary would have thought she was mad, and she must have been.

'The house is haunted. It is full of ghosts. There is a ghost of myself that has been here since long before I was born. *Have you ever seen it?*'

Poor Mary. Think what you were saved. It would have scared you to death. She tore the letter into small pieces.

That evening when it was growing dark, and Sybil was moving comfortably through the ground floor turning on lights and drawing curtains and talking to the cats, Jess was upstairs putting on a clean smock before Laurie came home. She stuck out a mile.

'You're wearing it very low,' Montgomery had said.

'Mind your own business.' He was only allowed to discuss things like the baby's name, or where it would go to school. Nothing professional. Jess was still going to her obstetrician in Boston, where the baby would be born.

Apart from her shape, she did not look too bad. She did not look so unformed and childish any more. Perhaps she was going to mature gracefully through motherhood. I like myself, she thought, looking into the same mirror where a year ago she had stared and stared and hated herself.

An experiment. She turned out the light in the room and in the upper hall, and took a risk.

'I'm glad she's dead,' she said aloud in the dim room. Then she stared and stared at herself in the mirror until her eyes swam and the lines of her reflection grew blurred. Moving like a sleep-walker, with her eyes fixed, she went out into the hall towards the place where she had first come face to face with a vision of herself.

Nothing. There could never have been anything. A fantasy which seemed ludicrous now as she walked right up against the empty wall where her face had hung, and laughed against the musty wallpaper.

15

ABOUT THE END of July, Roger began to talk again.

For two days, the threat of thunder had oppressed the air. Sybil was limp and querulous. Jess and the baby sweated in the homespun Pilgrim dress. The cats panted under bushes like dying stoles.

When the storm broke over the bay, great shafts of jungle rain came sweeping in to wash the yellow house, and a pail and basin made music all night under the two weak spots in the roof.

The parched earth, cracking like an old woman's skin, relaxed in dark brown fragrance. On the driveway, the birds took baths in puddles instead of the dust. The phlox revived, and Sybil felt so well that in the afternoon, she took Dorothy's secateurs out to trim off the shattered roses.

Japanese beetles, stronger than the wind and rain, were clinging to the dead heads, and eating their way disgustingly into the tight buds that had ridden out the storm. Dorothy used to spray them vindictively, murdering them as they gorged, gritting her teeth as she directed a specially vicious shot at the couples who were getting married on Henry Ford and Mrs Sam McGredy.

Rose spray. Sybil went to the toolshed, but the sprayer was empty. Dorothy used to mix powder in a bucket under the outside tap.

Sybil could see her clearly, vast from behind like a square triumphal arch, bending in the broad jeans. Where did she keep the powder? It was hard to remember, when people simply went off and left you trying to find where they put things. There should be a big jar like a gallon jar for Coca-Cola syrup somewhere. It didn't matter. Sybil stood vacant-eyed and slack-mouthed by the rose bed, trailing the empty sprayer.

'What's the matter?' Anna Romiza called through the open kitchen window.

'I wanted to spray the beetles.'

'What with?'

'Nothing.'

'You can use the spray can I got for the flies. I'll bring it out. Just wait while I dry my hands.'

'No dear, I'll come in. You've got your work, I've got mine.'

Always so thoughtful. In the old days, with Nancy and Walter, she would work right along with them, and Nancy said, pretending: 'I don't know what good we are, she'd never miss us.'

In the spring when it was bedding-out time, she and Nancy worked side by side up on the hill all day, and when Theo came up to see who was going to make dinner, he would say they were better than men. Nancy was like a man. She picked Sybil up once, and Theo said: 'That's more than I can do.' They laughed then. They were always laughing. Now there wasn't much to laugh at. When the

209

young ones threw away a joke and she asked them to repeat it, they said it wouldn't be funny any more, but then looked at each other and burst out laughing again, which showed it was.

April April laugh thy girlish laughter. 'What month is this, Anna?' When she went into the kitchen, she had forgotten what she came for. Poor Roger looked very droopy. He couldn't be moulting, if Anna was right about it being July. There was a roast in the oven and the kitchen was too hot.

'I'll take him out and hang him in a tree. He can imagine he's free and wild.'

'Why don't you let him go?' Anna asked.

'He'd get killed by the other birds.' Everybody knew that. Anna was a good friend, but she was very silly. You couldn't have a conversation with her. It passed through Sybil's mind and out the other side that she might tell Jess that she could manage on her own while she was out being a Pilgrim maid.

As Sybil was going out of the door, lopsided with the bird-cage, Anna said: 'I thought you came in for the spray.'

'Thank you,' Sybil concealed surprise with dignity.

While she was directing spray from the can at the beetles, aiming carefully, firing straight into the ruined heart of the rose where the obscene shellbacks clung, Dorothy said calmly: 'Sybil.'

'What have I done?' She wheeled round. Why shouldn't she use the can? But Dorothy wasn't there. She was hiding, playing tricks again. In the bushes. Behind a tree. Round the corner of the house. As soon as Sybil's back was turned, she would spring out and say Groo. Where are you, Dot? I know where you are.

'Sybil Sybil Sybil.'

Trembling, gasping, her heart knocking a tattoo, Sybil leaned against the tree and shook her fist weakly at the bird, whistling and chattering a whole string of old tag phrases, arching his wing muscles and agitating his plumage so that the cage swung on the low branch.

'HE'S TALKING AGAIN.' When Jess came home, she told her about it at once.

Jess stood under the cage and chirped to the bird and called him pretty names. He listened with his head tilted and his eye unblinking. He would not answer, but as soon as Sybil and Jess and Anna began to talk together, he started off with catch phrases, unreeling the inane old dialogue that he had picked up from Dorothy.

'I don't know that I can live with it,' Laurie said when he heard it. 'It's too unnervingly like her.'

'Perhaps she's pushed poor Henry out.' Jess tried to make a scared face, but she giggled. 'Perhaps her soul has come back into that bird.'

She was going to giggle again, but Sybil said: 'Yes. Yes, that's right. It has.' Why could they not see it? It was all so clear. Clear and simple and, as she saw now, inevitable.

They tried to jolly her out of it. Well, they could think what they liked, but she knew now. It was obvious. This was the way it had to be. In the following days, she became increasingly obsessed with the idea that Dorothy's spirit was in the bird. It was in her mind all day. She could not talk about it to the others, so she hardly spoke, for there was nothing else that she could talk about.

She grew confused again. Many times, she could not tell who was who. It was like those strange dream-like days with Dorothy on Emerson's bed, when she was not sure which was Dorothy and which was the bird.

Had that been a dream? No one ever talked about it. Emerson's door was locked, so she could not go in to see.

'Why has she locked herself in?' she asked Jess.

'Hush, Gramma dear.' The child patted her, as if she were the grandmother and Sybil the child. 'We took away the key.'

Were they all in league against her? Was that it? If they knew that Dorothy was in there, were they keeping Sybil out so that they could have her for themselves?

Dot was her friend. 'The best pal you ever had, Sybil Camden Prince,' she said, wagging her thick black head until the earrings swung like prayer bells. 'It was a lucky day for both of us when the road brought me to you.'

Dorothy was her friend, but they kept her locked away. The Dorothy bird was there, and Sybil took to spending most of her time in the kitchen, sitting at the table with her forearms slack and idle and her fingers fiddling with nothing, speaking her thoughts aloud for the bird to hear, and waiting for an answer.

'It give me the creeps,' she heard Anna say to someone, 'to see her sit there and converse with herself.' And Montgomery—that was who she said it to—came over and sat down opposite her at the table and held her hands to keep the fingers still, and made distracting conversation, when all she wanted to do was listen for the bird.

Sometimes it was silent for hours on end. Sometimes it

would chatter non-stop. You never knew, so you had to stick around. That was like Dot. Always keep 'em guessing. Good old Dot. Sybil did not know what she would have done without her in these muddled days. It was absurd of them to pretend not to believe she had come back. They were not as stupid as that. They did not want her to have Dorothy. But Dorothy was all she had, if everyone else was going to call her a liar.

'Hullo Sybil.'

When the bird said that, she would answer cheerfully: 'Hullo, Dot.'

Jess would screw up her face and say: 'Gramma, *please*,' but it was Dorothy's voice, after all, so why be rude?

If the minister came in here today (but they were keeping him away too), and said: 'Good morning, Mrs Prince' in his own voice, what would they say if she answered: 'Good morning, Maggie Riley'? They'd have her shackled to the walls in no time.

When Sybil talked about the Dorothy bird, Jess looked scared, and Anna cried: 'Jesus!' and glued her hand to her mouth. But there was nothing to be scared of. There was no fear any more.

What she could not make anybody understand—and she had not tried for fear of spoiling it—was that Dot had come back to her in peace. As a friend. As a protector. That was why she had come back, for Sybil was weak and helpless and did not know the score.

There was one day when Jess, who was usually so gentle, burst out to her: 'Don't keep on with this! You hated her! We shall rot in hell for letting her stay with you.'

'Get a hold on yourself, child,' Sybil said, very calmly,

213

leaning on her stick, her foot tapping, mistress of the affair. 'You'll make yourself ill.'

She could not understand, the flushed, tousled English girl, carrying her baby so awkwardly, for that art had gone out, along with needlepoint. Could not or would not understand.

Dorothy had come back as a friend. A protector. A lover.

If she had not promised Sybil, and herself, that she would stay here at least until her baby was born, Jess might have told Laurie that she could not go on with it.

But she had promised him too, and after their first appalled discussion of Sybil's hallucination, he had not wanted to talk about it again. It was trivia to him, women's chat to bore a man as soon as he got home. He shrugged it off, not irritably, but too lightly. The grandmother's harmless fancy. He humoured her, and said: 'Oh sure, sure,' without listening.

If Jess spoke of the bird, he humoured her too, patted her and gave her quick, sexless kisses, and said that everything would be all right when she had the baby to keep her busy.

Sybil was cute enough not to overdo the bird when Laurie was there, but the rest of the time, she was gruesomely obsessed.

As well as finding his voice again, Roger had found his

214

spirit of adventure. He had refused to leave the cage after Jess and Laurie captured him upstairs, but now he came out whenever Sybil opened the door. She would climb onto the chrome and plastic stool, teetering and gasping, and bring him out on her finger.

'Jess! Jess! Help me down!'

'You shouldn't get up there.' Jess held out her hand and took the old woman's weight as she half fell, clumsily, off the stool.

'Don't be sharp with me.' Sybil turned up her eyes in a sickening, doggy way.

'I only said you shouldn't climb up there,' Jess repeated in the controlled nursing home shout she despised, but could not avoid sometimes, if she were not to scream.

'She asked me to,' Sybil said smugly.

Roger had never stayed with Sybil for long when Dorothy was alive, but now he would perch on her shoulder for hours, nibbling in her hair like a woodpecker and whispering in her ear. Sybil would sit there with a silly, senile smile across her face and her teeth out, for she was forgetting the essentials, now that the bird ruled her life.

She even tried to betray the cats, for the black panther with the whiskers like piano wires had never forgotten his taste of Roger's tail feathers. He sat all day under the cage, slotting his eyes, his muscular tail lashing and curling with a life of its own. When Sybil sat at the table with the bird on her shoulder, the cat would appear in the opposite chair, bolt upright, like a husband waiting for a meal.

'I'm scared of him,' Sybil said. 'Look how he stares.'

'It's not you he's got in mind.' Jess smiled and caressed the cat, for she often wished that he would spring, and end it.

'He'll have to go,' Sybil said, in an odd flat voice, her eyes not focusing.

'Over my dead body.' But the bird was churring and whispering in Sybil's ear, and she was not listening.

It was very hot. Jess was beginning to have pains in her legs, and she spent more time sitting on a bench at the Plantation, hoping she would not be seen and told to circulate. The crowds and the heat and the baby grew, and she grew more tired, but she could not give it up, for her afternoons away from the house were the only sane part of the day.

She longed to get away, and dreaded coming back. When Anna left, there were at least two hours before Laurie came home. Sometimes she thought about killing the bird. Or taking him in her hand and throwing him out upon the air. What if he would not fly away? What if he came back, pecking at the window screens, tapping round the casement of the door? And she knew that she could not kill him and could not throw him away, because it would mean that she was deranged too, that she believed what Sybil believed.

There were forty-three of them, I counted. The day I was there, there were only thirty-nine.

Jess was on the stairs when the voices came to her again. She stopped halfway down, one foot below the other, the weight in front of her balanced on her bent knee, and listened to them.

They were selling them cheap. I hate to hurry you, but we have to leave in five minutes.

There were two of them, but in her own voice, and when one of them said: There's no excuse, the words seemed to pass in front of her eyes, not seen, yet perceived with another sense than hearing, like images on the inside of closed lids, although her eyes were open.

The voices did not come again, but she kept the radio on downstairs, and turned on the transistor in her room, loud enough to keep them away.

Two nights later, she asked Laurie: 'Do you believe it?'

'What?' They were lying on their backs, the moonlight on his face, her body a sheeted mound.

'What Sybil believes—about the bird.'

'Don't start that now. Get your sleep.'

'You shouldn't let her go on . . .'

'If it gives her pleasure. Why do you get so upset over the poor old lady? It isn't good for her, or you.'

'I can't stand it. I can't—' She almost said: I can't stay here, but caught her breath in a dry sob and said: 'I can't stand the bird any longer.'

He had closed his eyes, a marble face under the moon. He did not answer, but she saw his lips tighten.

She raised herself on her elbow. 'I want to get rid of it,' she whispered.

He opened his eyes and looked at her for an agonising moment as if she were nothing, nobody to him, before he smiled, and reached out a hand, and murmured: 'Come on now. If you're going to be like this every time you're pregnant, we'd better not have any more kids.'

In the misery that stayed with her all the next day, Jess walked in the garden after dinner, not able to go to bed, not able to sit in the room where Laurie was reading. Through the dusk, a light warm rain fell briefly, not wetting the grass or cooling the air, just passing over the garden like the shadow of a plane.

The crickets and the obsessive summer cars competed for her ears. She went through the gate in the fence, and as she walked up through the dry grass of the meadow, someone walked with her, half a step behind. There was no noise or movement of the grass, but her nerve ends were aware.

She was wearing a light pink dress, and in the corner of her eye, she saw the pale glimmer in the twilight which was almost gone. She quickened her pace, but you can't outrun your shadow. At the bank where the meadow rose more steeply to meet the trees, she turned with a sigh and went to meet it. She walked right through its solemn face and insubstantial dress and fell forward into the dry rank grass that the cows had left.

She tried to scream, but it was the paralysed screaming of a dream, jerked out of the sleeper no louder than a moan. She lay there for a long time, with grass in her open mouth like a mad woman. Then she knelt and watched the lights of the house, and at last she got up and began to go slowly back, keeping one hand in front of her to push away the dark.

She was going to Laurie, but when she reached the house, she went upstairs and got into the bed and fell heavily asleep as if she had been driven to exhaustion, or beaten.

SOME TIME LATER, she tackled Sybil.

'I have to ask you something, Gramma.'

'Ask away, my dear.'

'Come into the other room.'

'Why?'

She was not going to say: So Roger can't hear us. She was not going to be caught that way, playing Sybil's game.

Sybil followed her obediently, and Jess shut the door and faced her.

'Tell me something honestly. Do you think this house is haunted?'

'Well, my dear.' Sybil began to mumble her bruised lips in and out, tasting the words she might say. 'All houses are haunted, don't you know, by the folk who have lived in them.'

'You told me the first day I ever came here, you told me that there was a ghost of Ralph Waldo Emerson, and that you had heard him breathing. Remember telling me that?'

The old lady nodded, her eyes innocent, rinsed of colour by the years. 'I could have done that. You slept in Emerson's room, didn't you?' She brightened to a clearer memory. 'You were going to be married. He slept in there, you know, the night before his wedding to that Plymouth girl.'

'You told me. And then you told me that sometimes when you were in that room, you could hear him breathing on the bed.'

'Did I scare you?'

'Of course. I woke screaming in the night, don't you remember? And Laurie thought it was because I didn't want to be married. I tried to forget about it. Now I want to remember. Tell me more about that room. Tell me everything that ever happened. What you saw, what you heard.'

Sybil shook her head. 'Nothing, really.'

'But you told me—'

'Oh my dear,' Sybil looked down and smoothed her dress over her lap, 'an old woman's fancies. My Aunt Lilian Fugler saw a fairy once. I'll bet you never met anyone under seventy-five who saw a fairy.'

'You mean you made it up?'

Sybil nodded, still looking down and smoothing the cotton print over her knee, which trembled slightly.

'Why did you?'

'Just foolishness, I guess. I can't remember now. I used to imagine I heard him, to keep me company in there, nights when I watched the cars and couldn't sleep. It got to seem real.'

'But it was real! I heard him, Gramma. I swear to you I did. You told me the story, and I was afraid. I woke in the middle of the night, and there was someone lying beside me on the bed. I heard the breathing. You must have heard it too.'

Sybil looked confused. 'I can't remember.' Her fingers began to fiddle and pick at her dress, like dying hands plucking the sheets. 'I can't remember ever hearing a thing.'

'But I did.'

Sybil shrugged, collecting herself. 'That's your affair,' she said, and reached for her cane on the back of the chair.

'Don't go for a minute.' Jess took the cane and put it behind her back, standing close to the chair and looking down at Sybil. 'I want to ask you something else.'

'It's not my day for being asked questions,' Sybil grumbled. 'I can't remember things today.'

'Yes you can. You can remember once when I was in your room at bedtime, and I asked you if this house was haunted.'

'What did I say?' Sybil asked with interest, waiting for the answer with her mouth open.

'You didn't deny it. You were going to tell me something, and then Dorothy came in and interrupted and I thought perhaps you were afraid to say anything in front of her.'

'Scared of Dot?' Sybil glanced towards the kitchen and smiled. 'You're getting fanciful, Miss Jess. It usually happens in the earlier months.'

'Think back to being in bed. It was your birthday. I gave you that dressing-gown with the rosebuds, the one you spilled grape soda on. Can't you remember what you were going to say?'

'About what?' Sybil was losing course, sidetracked by grape soda.

'About the house being haunted.'

'Oh that.'

'You told me that you had seen a ghost.'

'Did I?' Sybil spread her hands and said easily: 'Don't take too much notice of that, my dear. Old people see ghosts all the time, you know. Those that have gone are still with us in memory. Though lost to sight, to memory dear thou ever wilt remain. You see, I don't forget things. My Papa used to read poetry to me by the hour, you know. He had his favourites; well, we all do. I have mine . . .' She began to ramble, her eyes in the past, her mouth slack.

'You said you had seen a ghost,' Jess repeated, holding herself tense, gripping the handle of the cane in her effort to will the old lady into sense. 'Think back. Think. Did you—did you ever see a ghost of me?'

221

'How could I, honey?' Sybil turned and smiled up at her. 'You're not dead.'

'I mean, before you knew me. Before I ever came here.'

'Oh sure.'

So it was true. Jess stared at her, but Sybil was still smiling fondly. 'All grandmas do, I guess. I used to dream of the girl my Laurie would marry. I always hoped it would be someone like you. A nice girl, pretty and kind. You've been kind to me, Jess. You're a good girl.'

Jess gave her back her stick, but Sybil did not get up. 'What did you want to ask me?' she asked intelligently. 'You wanted to ask me something.'

'I have. I wish I hadn't,' Jess added softly, as she moved away.

Out of the tangle of illogic and wool-gathering, one truth remained. No one but Jess had ever seen a ghost in this house.

Even poor Mary, with all her myths and legends, and the Charity tree weeping under the new moon. Shall I write to her again and ask her if that too was a lie? And she will answer Yes, and say it was only hysteria, from the servant's mumbo jumbo. And I shall know for certain then. This house is haunted only for me.

'WOULD YOU LIKE a drink, Gramma?'

'Shan't we wait for Laurie?'

'He's not coming tonight. Remember, I told you.'

(They always said that, but it wasn't necessarily true.) 'He's going to hear the Vice-President speak and go on to the reception, and he'll stay the night in town.'

'Not taking his wife to the party?'

'Look at her.' Jess stuck her stomach out even farther and made a face like a pig. They both laughed.

Jess made mint juleps, and Sybil said: 'In my day, no mother would dream of taking liquor for the whole nine months.'

'In my day, no mother would last the nine months without it.'

They laughed again. The girl was friendly and more cheerful. She seemed to have got over her odd fit earlier in the day when she kept asking Sybil something and Sybil could not seem to give her the right answer, which was not surprising, since she was never quite clear what the question was.

The day was waning in unremitting heat. It was cooler in the house, so they sat in the shaded back room, and Sybil brought the Dorothy bird to share the pleasant hour with her, and perch on the edge of the wooden bowl, drilling holes in the potato chips. It would not surprise Sybil to see it take a peck into her julep. Dorothy had liked her shot.

'You make a very fair julep, child. Just like we always had them.' The medicinal bitter sweetness, half taste, half fragrance, was like a sob for so many other summers. Juleps with Theo while the tired figures on the hillside moved slowly, raking the last of the hay before dark. Parties for John—or was it Laurie?

'Uncle Ted taught me.'

Parties for Ted. He had betrayed that girl with the funny nose like a faucet. 'Everyone knew about it. There

223

was quite a scandal. I expect she's dead now.' She chuckled. It was comic to think of everyone else falling apart but Sybil.

She raised her glass, and the bird said without looking at her: 'Drink up Sybil, drink up. Sybil Sybil Sybil.'

Jess made a face at the bird, and Sybil said: 'He always said that when Dot gave me medicine. Stuff she'd made herself.'

'I always wondered why you drank it.'

'I had to.' Sybil glanced at the bird, but he was investigating under his wing. 'There was no gainsaying her. You know that. Drink up, she'd say, and I did.' She put up a hand between her mouth and the bird and whispered to Jess behind it: 'Though I'll admit to you now that there was a time when I was afraid she was trying to poison me.'

Weird—that came back all of a sudden. She had forgotten about that time of terror, since Dorothy came back to the world so benign. 'I thought she drugged my hot milk.' She could see herself now, sitting at the table, crying because she dared not drink and dared not refuse. It was all coming back. Must be the mint.

'Poor Gramma,' Jess said, not really believing. 'But then in the end, she poisoned herself. You don't suppose she meant that batch of pills for you?'

'Oh no,' Sybil said quickly, 'Oh no, because she didn't make those pills. She was much too sick.'

'I'm coming down.' She looked up in fear, and Dorothy loomed against the banister rail, wild-haired, lipstick on her teeth, her face as red as her awesome robe, the wide arc of raspberry buttons done up all wrong. The rack of coughing seized her and she gripped the rail until it shook, and the thin wooden posts trembled.

Sybil thought she would choke to death. When Dorothy raised her head, her eyes were streaming, and saliva ran from her scarlet mouth onto the scarlet robe.

'God damn it,' she said—Dorothy never swore—'I'll never make it.'

'I'll do it, Dot.' Sybil heard herself gabbling and falling over her words, so eager to help. 'I'll make the pills. I know how. I've helped you dozens of times.'

'Tell me how,' Dorothy croaked, suspicious in extremis.

'You take the powder, the parsnip root, and mix it with the bilberry pulp, and then you pound in cornmeal and put in a mess of honey till it tastes good, and then you roll the pills.'

Clever Sybilla, Dorothy could have said, but she only grunted: 'O.K. I guess you can do it. It's the only thing will do me any good.'

The jelly jars in which Dorothy kept the powders and liquids she used were on the top shelf of the cupboard, neatly labelled, for Dorothy was as precise in her herbalism as John Camden had ever been.

Sybil could not find her reading glasses, had not been able to find them for days, but she knew which was the jar for the dried parsnip root. A place for everything and everything in its place was one of Dorothy's sayings, informatively, as if no one else had ever said it.

There it was, next to the horseradish. It was tall and narrow and had once held dill pickle chips. Sybil stood on a chair, panting and clutching at the cupboard shelves. The jar was empty.

What now? She sat down on the chair holding the empty pickle jar, facing the counter under the cupboard as if she were going to play the organ. The eye of the mind saw a tiny figure of herself, like things seen far away in

225

fever, limping up the stairs, knocking on Dorothy's door and saying: 'I'm sorry, Dot. I couldn't do it.'

Impossible. She had to do it. She had promised. And Dorothy would be pleased with her. She would say: I owe you my life, Sybil Camden Prince, because Sybil had not failed her in her time of greatest need. Sybil had made pills.

But the wild parsnip. She had not been up to the old seedhouse on the nursery hill for at least a year, but she knew that was where Dorothy dried the various roots on the sunny shelves, and beat them into powder and stored them in big jars she got from the lady at the soda fountain. This lady's name was Ethel Wills, and she ate only Nature's foods like dandelion salads and carrot tops, which made it hard for her to have to work among the synthetic juices and plastic hot dogs, but easy for her to understand about the herbal remedies, and so she saved the big syrup jars for Dorothy.

Thinking of Ethel Wills, and the hot fudge sundaes they had enjoyed from her, and would enjoy again when Dorothy was well, Sybil changed her shoes without realising just what she was about, and found herself out on the wet spring lawn, headed for the gate of the fence.

There had been a path once, a dirt track for the brown horse that hauled the cart, and later Theo's tractor, and the Jeep. Trees and bushes were gradually obliterating it, seeded firs growing up between the ruts. Dorothy would not use the path, because the branches caught at her hair. Was it a wig? The thought arrested Sybil as she wandered in the trees on the other side of the fence, looking for the path. Or did Dorothy prefer to climb up through the meadow, because it was too steep for Sybil to follow?

She headed back to the grass, chopping angrily with her

cane at thistles, which did not flinch. I was running up that hill long before you were born, she told whoever it was who was telling her it was too far. I'll get up, she panted aloud, stumbling and lurching through the lumps and tufts the winter had heaved, if I have to do it on my hands and knees. And later, after a blank interval when there was no mind to think or speak with, only a body toiling perpetually upward, she came to herself in sunlight and saw that she was indeed climbing the last slope on hands and knees.

Her cane was gone, somewhere far below. Who cares. I lose one a week. Stones were under her hands, dry cow-dung, thistles. She raised her head like a tortoise and saw the top of the seedhouse, leaning against the sky, its old blue paint faded and flaked like a dinghy left too long in the water.

Excelsior. In New Hampshire, Papa took her up a mountain, and they said Excelsior to each other when they reached the top. But there was another top farther on, and so they said it again there.

Rasping breaths knifed her throat. She paused, leaning against the slope, and decided not to go any farther. It had been a good climb. Below her, the house sat quietly among the bare trees, waiting for the leaves to clothe it. It was very peaceful resting here on the bosom of her own hill, with a small breeze softening her face that had been climbing with clenched jaw. Perhaps she should stay here. Here at the quiet limit of the world, Papa said, under the sky, with the dark miles of pines between him and the sea. Here at the quiet limit of the world, a white haired shadow roaming like a dream the ever-silent spaces of the East.

But he never did roam here. He went away and left

her with Marma. Wait for me, Papa! With a grunt, she pushed herself upright and moved one foot above the other, to find him at the top of the hill.

The door of the seedhouse was shut, but not locked. She pushed in and sat down on the broken chair, getting her breath back in the familiar dusty savour of dried earth and flowerpots and crumbled herbs.

I did it. I did it, Dot. You will be proud of me.

After a while, she was able to get up and poke about on the shelves, looking for what she had come for. But she knew what she had come for, that was the thing. They thought she was done for, obsolete, a useless crone sopping her crusts in sweet tea.

There were roots spread on the drying racks. Some of them had been there too long and were mildewing, some were crumbled and hollow. No telling what they were, but they were no use anyway. On a shelf at the back of the shed, near the thick board and the scarred rolling pin that Dorothy used to crush roots and dried stalks were the big jars that Ethel Wills gave her. Sybil took the one that contained the most powder, since Dorothy would need a good supply of pills to tide her through convalescence, and clutching it to her, shut the door of the shed and went home the longer way down the road and down the driveway, using a bamboo plant stake for a cane.

As she mixed up the powder and the fruit pulp and the cornmeal in the old wooden bowl, she wished that Dorothy could see her, so efficient. But if Dorothy were there, she would be doing the mixing. Sybil was only allowed to roll the pills.

She tipped in an amber waterfall of honey. She added a little more, for Dorothy's sweet tooth, and hooked in a finger nail, to taste before she rolled. Disgusting. Did the pills always taste that bad? If so, Dorothy had been putting a good face on them to shame Sybil for grimacing over the willowleaf wine.

But poor old Dot was sick now, and must be pampered. When Mary was a child, you couldn't get a pill down her, hysterical as she was. Polly used to hide her tablets in a big spoonful of strawberry preserve. They still had some of Melia's chunky marmalade, for when oranges were cheap, she had made enough for a year's siege. When she had rolled the pills, Sybil took them upstairs with the marmalade and a spoon and a glass of water on a tray. She had to lay the marmalade jar on its side, and the water was all over the tray by the time she reached the top, but she filled up the glass in the bathroom and knocked on Emerson's door.

'Where have you been?' Dorothy jerked open the door as if she had been waiting behind it. 'I thought you'd died.'

'I might have,' Sybil said proudly, 'with my heart. Going all—'

But Dorothy would not hear the epic tale. She grabbed a pill, chased it down with water and began to cough again, holding the sides of her great chest as if the bows of her ribs might fly apart.

Sybil put the tray on a chair and put two pills into a big spoonful of marmalade, and when Dorothy opened her mouth to gasp, Sybil popped in the spoon, opening her own mouth like a mother feeding a baby.

Dorothy leaned against the doorpost and glowered wanly. 'That marmalade tastes funny.'

'Best in the house!' She did not remind her who made it, for Dorothy could never hear any good of Melia Mulligan, only bad. 'Take a couple more, for luck. That's a good girl. Come on now, to please Sybil.' Cooing and

229

coaxing, for there was no more ire in Dorothy, only a sickly weakness, she gave her two more marmaladed pills, and was emboldened to suggest: 'Let me help you back into bed.'

The slam of the door wiped the smile from her face like the back of a hand.

'WHY DIDN'T YOU tell us this before?'

'I never thought about it. All the fuss and excitement and the fool questions, it went clean out of my head. Can you imagine me making it to the seedhouse and down? I couldn't do it now to save my life. But to save Dot's, I could.'

She was losing logic again, quite serenely, but Jess was beginning to tremble. She felt sick and cold, and her hands were shaking, so she twisted them together. They were sweating, but her mouth was thick and dry and it was hard to speak.

'It must have been the shock of—the shock of—' She could not speak to Sybil about Dorothy's death.

She did it. She killed her.

She put her hands to her mouth and rushed out of the room. She ran outside, though the sink was nearer, and vomited up her soul into the long feathery grass beside the wire of the tennis court. There was nothing left inside her, and the baby plunged fretfully, as if he too would be vomited up and leave her.

230

She lay there for a long time. When she got up at last and carried the baby indoors on legs that had no power, Sybil seemed to have forgotten everything again. She had poured herself another drink, and was in the kitchen chopping cabbage with the glass at her elbow, like any suburban housewife cooking dinner by the light of a martini.

'What's the matter, child?' She turned as Jess came in. 'You look terrible.'

'How do you expect me to look?' Jess swallowed, to see if she might be sick again.

'It's hard, I know. It's hard for women. Dot says if men had to have the babies, it would solve the population problem.' She laughed. 'Shall I put dill into the slaw, or does it get in your teeth the way it does mine?'

She had forgotten already. Whatever door had kept the truth concealed had clanged again. Jess was the only one who knew.

Let me forget too, she prayed before she went to sleep. Let me forget. But in the leaden awakening of the morning, what might have been a dream was true.

She could hardly look at Sybil. When she took in the breakfast tray, and the old lady reached out scarecrow arms to embrace her, Jess stepped back quickly to the window, pretending to look out. She killed her. She stared down into the garden in a panic. She let her die an agonising death. She's a murderess. She's mad.

All day the thoughts twisted in her mind like maggots. She spent most of the morning in bed. Then she telephoned Anna and asked her to come early. She drove to where a finger of rocks lay out into the sea, and sat hunched up in her Pilgrim dress, staring at the green shifting water, not caring that the people who were fishing on the rocks farther out stared at her white Dutch cap and her big white collar fluttering.

She craved the crowded obliteration of the Plantation, but when it was time to go there, she could not show them her face. She went back up the beach, carrying her shoes, and got into the car and drove barefoot towards Boston. When she was in the street where Laurie's office was, she could not get out of the car because she was wearing her Pilgrim dress, so she drove back to Camden House and asked Anna if she would stay on for a while.

She changed her clothes and sat outside behind a tree, and when she heard Laurie's car at the top of the steep driveway, she rushed round the house to cry to him: She killed her! But when he stopped the car with a bounce and jumped out and ran to her, she could not tell him.

She had asked Anna to stay later, because she had the idea that when she told Laurie, he would take her away from there. Away from Sybil and the bird and the yellow house and the stench of death that swept down the stairs like poison gas.

He put his arm around her and they went into the house together, and nothing was changed. She could not change it. If she told Laurie—but torturing everyone would not make her own torture less. Suppose he felt a perverted legal compulsion to reveal the truth, even about his own grandmother? Montgomery? His doctor's code could also righteously destroy. Nothing to gain by haggling over Dorothy's disintegrating corpse. Everything to lose.

Sybil had forgotten already. The guilt had been passed to Jess. And to her child. She would tell him in the end, because she would tell him everything she knew. Laurie would bring him up in warm pride of his family. Then Jess would shiver it with her cold secret.

Somehow she got through another day. She went to the Plantation in the long woollen dress, which was strained now as tightly as Dorothy's cardigans. New images of Dorothy crowded her mind to replace the old false images of Dorothy as fool and fated bungler, hatching her own death. Dorothy was victim now, the bludgeoned corpse in Epping Forest, the mutilated woman in the river.

A victim who would never be avenged, because of Jess. She sat on a three-legged stool inside the Myles Standish House and held onto her baby and thought: I am not fit to have a child.

Myles Standish, with fiery ginger hair like scrubbing bristles glued too tightly to his head for wanton visitors to pluck, was doing business with one Hobomock in a Masonic apron, who brought beaver skins shaped like tennis rackets.

In the background, Rose Standish, a thin, work-weary woman with a furious wax baby, offered the Indian a plate of what looked like dog food, although you could tell by her harrowed face that it was her own dinner.

Visitors came in and out from the dusty sunlight, and asked questions and made the same joke about Mrs Standish and the dog's dinner, and Jess answered them automatically and laughed her polite Pilgrim laugh. A middle-aged woman in patchwork Bermuda shorts stood tiptoe girlishly to whisper something to her husband.

He looked at Jess. 'Quite right,' he said, as they went out. 'They had to populate America, after all.'

As she drove home, dark thunder clouds were massing over the bay, and by the time she reached the house, the light had gone out of the sky, and the air was holding its breath for rain. Anna ran to her car, for she hated to be in this house in a storm, waiting for a tree to crash through the roof.

The thunder stayed far off, rolling over the sea, but the rain began to fall, straight and heavy, thudding on the shingles. Upstairs, the bedroom was in twilight. It was hard to breathe. Rain was sluicing in from a broken gutter. Jess shut the window and turned to see herself in the long mirror behind the door.

She stood with her hot hands hanging awkwardly, a vast unwieldy bundle in the drab dress, an old face peering under the silly bonnet, a clumsy ugly person who would never be a girl again.

She turned on the light. As she moved about the room, her bulky reflection was everywhere, on the door, in the dressing-table mirror, on the window pane against the streaming dusk.

'Jess! Where are you?'

'In here.' Let her hear or not hear. I can't be in a room with her alone. A door shut, and Sybil's feet scraped unevenly across the hall and began to creak on the stairs.

Jess stood still. The sound of the closing door, the direction of the shuffle—it sounded just as if Sybil had come from Emerson's room. It had been locked since the men broke up the bed, threw it out of the window and burned it. Had she found the key? Was she compelled to haunt that dreadful room, without remembering why?

Jess waited until the stair treads were silent. Downstairs, Sybil sang out to the bird in a hymnal tremolo. I have got to know that she can't go in there. I can't go out of this room and past that door and turn towards the stairs, without knowing that it is locked.

Still in the Pilgrim dress, she went down the passage and across the corner of the hall. The closed door tilted slightly away from the hinge. She stood before it and looked at it for some time, vacantly, without expression. Then she put out her hand and turned the dull brass knob.

The door was not locked. She pushed very gently, and it opened, a little wider, wide enough to show her the fingers outstretched to meet hers on the cold door handle, the person in the humble white cap and stuffy dress, slim, neat at the waist.

With a cry she snatched away her hand and the door swung wide and would have banged against the bed, but there was nothing there.

My baby?

She flung out her hands. The image held out empty hands before an empty body.

My baby!

She was stabbed through with a terrible sensation of loss, as if her child were being torn from her, not skilfully, surgically, but roughly, brutally, in unbearable pain.

As she sank to her knees in the doorway, she saw the image sink with her, less clear now, greyly transparent, and they toppled forward together in a despairing embrace, and became one in pain.

When she opened her eyes, the image was gone. Between suffocating waves of pain, somehow she crawled to the railing above the stairs.

'Gramma! Gramma!' Music was playing below. She would not hear.

'What is it, child?' The face swam palely below. The mouth fell open as she saw Jess lying against the rail of the stair-well. 'I'll come up.'

'Get Mont. The hospital—' She heard herself begin to scream.

The next time she opened her eyes, Sybil was sitting

235

beside her on the floor, her back against the railing, legs straight out, very composed, cradling her to her sparse bosom.

'He's coming,' she said matter-of-factly.

'Soon?' It came out as a moan.

'I know, I know. Hang on, child. I know what it's like,' she said very sensibly. 'Gramma's here. Hang on.'

16

'SHE FELL,' SYBIL said. 'I found her on the floor. "Help me", she said, "help me".'

It made a good story, with herself as heroine. She had already told it half a dozen times to Mrs Thatcher, who was taking care of her while Jess was in the hospital, and would tell it again, if she so pleased. The woman was paid to listen to her.

Mrs Thatcher was a nurse, though it was years since she had been part of a bustling hospital routine. She had her name written on a blue and silver plaque over her breast pocket: Mrs C. L. Thatcher, in case you were a crazed old lady and could not remember who she was.

She wore white overalls, buttoned high at the neck like a dentist, and as flat in the front as a dentist, which was a change from Dorothy's pouter pigeon architecture. She had white stockings which had caught a few patches of blue dye in the washing machine, and great white shoes like South Sea liners, with little portholes round the toes to let out the sweat.

Sybil rather liked her. She was kind, in a businesslike

way, for old ladies were her business, rather than her cross. She did not make Sybil feel a nuisance. That was a change too. She had been cluttering up people's lives for so long that it was a relief to be with someone who had all the time in the world for Sybil, and nothing else to do.

It was a little dull for Mrs Thatcher at Camden House, so from time to time Sybil livened things up by hiding in the garden, or locking herself in the bathroom and pretending she could not open the door.

Mrs Thatcher did not lose her temper. Her bull moose face had been set on patient planes years ago, and could not tilt towards emotion. Her patience was limitless. You could not disconcert her. She said Yes dear and No dear and Holy Mother Church. Conversationally she was very poor.

But the Dorothy bird made up for that. It was talking more than ever these days, and if Sybil did not open the door of the cage as soon as she came downstairs, it would rattle the bars with its strong hooked beak until Mrs Thatcher remarked without raising her head that the ceiling would come down.

The bird spent most of the day either perching upon Sybil or near her. Sometimes it messed on her dress, and Mrs Thatcher would bring a warm wet sponge, before it left a mark. It was handy to have someone like that around, dressed as a dentist, to take care of those little jobs that Sybil used to leave for weeks, or forget for ever, before she had Mrs Thatcher to wait on her and the bird.

With the fire lighted in the first cool evenings, it was cosy sitting in her own chair with a glass of the tonic wine Mrs Thatcher prescribed, the bird on her shoulder, making kissing sounds and whispering familiar nonsense in her ear. Where's the money get the telephone bedtime

Sybil Sybil Roger kiss Mother. Just as cosy as it used to be sitting here with Dorothy when the day had gone well and she was in a good mood. The bird was always in a good mood, which was an improvement. It still coughed, and Sybil would say: 'You've got to cut down on those cigarettes, Dot,' and laugh indulgently, for she never would.

'DON'T THINK I'M complaining,' Mrs Thatcher said to Jess, although it would not matter if she was, since she was leaving next week, and had another old lady lined up. 'I've heard some weird fancies in my life—well, it's my job, see—but never yet the transmigration of souls.'

'The bird?'

Mrs Thatcher nodded, just her chin, since the high collar held her neck at right angles to the floor. 'I don't want to worry you, just out of hospital and all, but she seems to think a friend of hers . . . I mean, she actually talks to it as if it were a person, if you know what I mean.'

'Oh, that's nothing. We've lived with that for ages.' Jess laughed, and sat down quickly, for she suddenly found she could not stand up any longer.

'Holy Mother Church,' said Mrs Thatcher. 'No wonder you had a prem.' The seven-months baby girl was still in the hospital, where she would have to stay for another month. Laurie was taking Jess away for a few days, which was all the firm would allow him, and when

239

they came back, costly Mrs Thatcher would go, and Sybil—

'How are we going to tell her?'

'Tell her while I'm in here,' Jess had said in the hospital,' but he could not. Sybil still thought that they would all go on living at Camden House together, as they had before. No one had told her that Jess and Laurie would be going back to Boston, and the house shut up for the winter. Jess had sobbed, even before Laurie had seen the tiny baby in the incubator: 'I can't live there. I won't.'

'Hush, hush.' Young and restless and colourful in the negative room, he made soothing noises at her, as if she were the newborn one. 'Not now, darling. We'll talk later.'

He stroked her limp hair, but she kept on: 'I can't stay there. Don't make me.'

She murdered Dorothy. She murdered Dorothy. She murdered Dorothy. The voice beat like drums in her head. She stared at him, surprised that he could not hear.

'I saw a ghost.'

'Hush love, it's all right. It's all over now. It was a dream. You must have fallen and passed out. Sybil said—'

'I saw a ghost. Mont knows. He believes me. Ask him.'

After it was finished, the terror and the pain, and Mont was no longer the God figure, sole saviour, but just Mont with a bit of hair sticking up at the back, lifting his big feet carefully into the room to see if she was awake, he had said: 'Well, I won.'

She nodded. It would be easy to cry.

'I told you I'd deliver your baby, though I didn't plan it quite like that. What happened, Jess? Sybil said she found you on the floor. What happened?'

'I saw a ghost.'

He pulled his mouth down sideways, considering this.

'I saw a ghost of myself.' He did not seem to think she was raving, so she told him about the image which belonged to her and yet had its own being. She told him about the bickering voices, and about the thing that glimmered beside her through the meadow.

'How long has this been going on?'

She shook her head. It did not matter. 'Where's Laurie?'

'On his way. They couldn't find him at first. I wanted to head him off from going home and having his grandmother meet him with tales of disaster.'

'She was very good.'

'She would be. That old lady has guts.'

'She killed Dorothy, you know.'

'Oh rats,' Montgomery said. 'Though I'll bet there were times when she wanted to.'

THE DAY AFTER they came back to Camden House, Dorothy's sister arrived without warning, at lunchtime.

'What do you want?' Laurie blocked the doorway, holding half a sandwich.

'I want to come and talk to you.'

'I'm sorry. My wife is just out of hospital. It's not convenient.'

'It's convenient to me,' said Mrs Hubbard, and he had

241

to step aside for her, or she would have pushed him flat and walked right on in over his chest and face.

Sybil was in the kitchen. Mrs Hubbard nodded to her, and Sybil nodded back pleasantly, and said: 'If it's the church collection, I—'

'I'd like to talk to you in private, Mr Brookes. Dorothy's sister went through the room without a word to Jess. Behind her back, Laurie shrugged and spread his hands, and followed her through to the front of the house.

Jess went upstairs and stayed there until Laurie came to find her.

'What did she want?'

'Trouble.' He made a face. 'She's been on to the police again, though I don't think they'll bother with her. It's an obsession. She won't believe that Dorothy killed herself.'

'What will you tell the police if they come here?'

'The truth.'

'Would you lie in court?'

'As a defence counsel, I might push facts around a bit. In the witness box, no. It's not worth it.'

'Would you tell me to lie?'

'Of course not.'

'Suppose she knows something. Suppose she goes on with it. Gets lawyers, forces the thing into court. Would you let me stand up and tell everybody your grandmother was a murderer?'

'Now don't you start.'

She jumped up and faced him with her fists clenched. 'She is! She did it! She killed her. She made those pills. She told me.'

'Nonsense,' Laurie said. 'You're making it up.'

Why did they all think that? 'It's true, she killed her.'

242

'I don't believe you,' he held her wrists, for she looked as if she were going to hit him.

'Ask her then. Go on down and ask her.'

'All right.' He let her go, pushing her backward onto the bed, and she lay there with her fist in her mouth and thought: Oh God, what have I done?

THEY DID NOT know she had the key to Emerson's room. They did not know she was that smart. But if they were no smarter than to hang it with all the others which fitted nothing on the back of the cellar door, labelled E's Room, then they had it coming to them.

A magpie, Mrs Thatcher called her, when she found all the candy and buttons in her handkerchief drawer, with the pieces of clamshell the gulls had dropped. She did not find Dorothy's tinkly earrings. She was quite a stupid woman, although she gave a dandy pedicure.

No one knew that she went into the front room at night and made the several faces of a witch at the cars. On the Friday of the Labour Day weekend, the cars went by in an endless last chance stream, and Sybil spent what seemed like most of the night kneeling at the window-sill. There was no companionable breathing at her back. They had taken away the bed. She had got into trouble for telling them about Emerson, and they had taken away the bed so that she could not tell it any more.

Dorothy's bed. Where was she sleeping now? *Doro*thee,

where are you *sleep*ing now? If I didn't kill her, who did? It's very distressing. Laurie shouldn't make me talk about it. It's over. All troubles fade when the day is done, sink into peace with the setting sun.

They'll send me away, you'll see, she told the chain of headlights that made a funnel of day on the highway and swept the trees incessantly awake. But I shan't go. I'll run away.

The next day, she ran, limping and falling and cutting her knees, over the beech-tree roots and down through the pasture, running to the barn where there was peace and the sweet wet breath of cattle.

'Where are you going, love?' Laurie came up casually behind her, a foxtail grass in his mouth.

'To the barn.'

'Come on.' He took her arm. 'I'll take you round there in the car.' He helped her back slowly, and they got in his car and drove over the bridge and down the cart track to the red barn, but all the cows were out at pasture, and there was no one there she knew.

'When is she going?' Mont asked.

'Tomorrow.'

'Does she know?'

'You can't tell. Sometimes she only pretends to forget.'

'You know it's the right thing, Laurie.'

'I don't want to talk about it.'

'I didn't come to talk about it anyway,' Mont said. 'I came to talk about the ghost.'

'No.' Laurie glanced at Jess and shook his head.

'Yes. I went into the Medical Library yesterday and looked something up. Want to hear about it?' he asked, as they were both silent.

'I don't think—'

'It explains a lot of things. Autoscopic phenomena, they call it. It's commoner than you'd think. I had heard of it vaguely, but never of an actual case. What you saw, Jess—it was always yourself, right?'

'I told you. Just a face once. Then more of the ghost. And then—'

'It wasn't a ghost. It was you, outside yourself. You project a double image of yourself. A sort of escape, peopling the world with you. Same with the voices, and when you heard the breathing. You were hearing yourself. There was a case of a man who lost his leg and then saw himself coming through a door without a limp. A woman who saw her double when she came back from her husband's funeral, because she didn't want to be alone.'

'But why me? I'm not like that. I'm sane. I'm normal. I'm not a case.'

'But you'll have to admit,' Mont said, not looking at either of them, 'you have been unhappy, and desperately upset at times this last year.'

'How do you know?'

'Oh, listen—'

'We were both unhappy,' Laurie said slowly. 'There were clouds of anger. I couldn't break through them.'

'It was Dorothy.' Jess glanced round, as if she might be in the room. 'Evil came in. I told you, Laurie. Evil came in with—'

Slashing through the steady background roar of the weekend traffic, the shriek of tyres brought them all to their feet.

SYBIL LOOKED AT the bird and the bird looked down at her, sideways, first with one eye, then hopping round on his perch to view her with the other.

The door was open, but he had not been out of his cage for two days. 'Come on, come to Sybil then.' But he would not speak. He had not spoken for two days.

'Did I dream it?' she asked him, but he was just a budgerigar. Roger, was his name. The Dorothy bird was gone. She had killed Dorothy, and they had all gone away and left her. Laurie and Jess and Montgomery had gone off in the front room and shut the door, bang, just as she was starting through the hall to join them.

Well, there it was. She stood irresolute in the middle of her kitchen. She had got so used to people telling her the next move at any given moment that when they all went away and left her alone, she did not know what to do.

The cars on the road were like the singing of blood in the ears. Someone thinking of me. Tell me a number. A, B, C, D . . . . *orothy*

Behind her, Dorothy said huskily: 'Come on, Sybil.'

No! She ran, dragging her foot, knowing that Dorothy was behind her, with blood red nostrils and lipstick on her fangs. Out over the lawn, stooping to push through the veil of the weeping beech, gasping in the little green cave, her hand on the safe grey hide. A rustling of the leaves— who's there! She struggled out through the other side, and ran zigzag from tree to tree, touching them, stumbling over the roots.

Papa! Pinafore strings flying, she ran down into the gentle valley to find him going ahead of her up to the barn with the cows. Wait for me, Papa! The wire fence tore at her clothes, and she staggered blindly up the slope, her eyes straining at the dusk to see him swinging a stick among the brown and white cattle. Wait for me!

The car struck, and tossed her like a bundle of rags back to the side of the road.

'It was the damnedest thing. The damnedest thing. I guess I—I thought I saw—it's crazy—I thought I saw— cows wandering across the highway.'

'Light's tricky, this time of day.' No one wanted to condemn.

'He's been eight hours on the road,' the driver's wife said. 'We'd better get you to a doctor, honey.'

AFTER THEY HAD taken Sybil away, and there was nothing more to do, Jess went into the kitchen to kill the bird.

But he was dead on the floor of his cage, lying on his back, his claws curled, his breast stuck up like a pouter pigeon.